Manor

Bea Lancaster

Book Cover by Bea Lancaster

ISBN: 9798371545985

Previously published as a KindleVella story in 2022.

To my mom who never stopped believing in me, and supports me in all my trials and errors. Thank you for being the best human!

June

Chapter One

A single hand pressed against the glass of a vintage Rolls Royce, as five people traveled down the backroads of Clinch County, Georgia. The rain was falling, and the swamplands were lapping it up. One person, in particular, who wasn't *lapping it up* in the backseat was Melody. Her hand slid down from the window, as she looked to her left at her friend Ashley. Ashley was never the wiser as she was nose-deep into a new novel: *Fahrenheit 451*.

"How do you not get car sick reading that?" Melody's nose scrunched up to even thinking about the idea of reading one of *those*. Her brown eyes semi-closed to showcase her disgust.

"I don't know. I guess I do it so much it doesn't bother me anymore. You'd like this though!" Ashley's doe-like eyes lit up at the possibility of getting her friend to read anything that wasn't about true crimes and death.

"Yea, yea, yea. That's what you always say, but I never get past the first few pages," Melody said as she rolled her eyes.

"That's because you don't give anything a chance, darling." Melody's mother, Patrice, quipped before going back to her phone to read the gossip. She was in her early forties, but one couldn't tell by looking at her. Her freshly french manicured nails clicked against the screen of the latest iPhone. They were nails that had never seen a day of work in their life. A rare breed of blue blood that never quite understood the toils of low class, and Melody wanted to be anything but her.

Melody looked out the window again, and all could see for miles were weeping trees and marshes. The houses turned from trailer parks to two-story homes, and she knew they were getting closer. Closer to her late father's manor that was passed down through generations, and then to him in a will by an estranged grandfather. When Dan passed, the manor was signed to Patrice–who hated the manor when Dan was alive. Patrice had decided that she would finally use it as a place to host a summer party.

"I can't believe it's been eight years since I've been here," Melody accidentally said out loud.

"And the first time with us all together as a family," said an arrogant voice from the front seat. It was a voice Melody hated more than anything: Melody's new stepfather, Robert.

"Family? I don't think that's the right word." Melody snapped back. "You are not *my* family."

"Melody!" Patrice shrieked. "You apologize to Robert right now!" Her slender finger pointed at them both.

"Sorry, Robert," Melody moaned as she fell back into her seat. Her brown hair was beginning to be wrapped by her finger.

"Thank you, Melody, you know I now see you as my daughter," Robert looked back at her while placing his arm on the seat top. He had slightly longer hair towards the front that led to a fade. The strands fell in front of his eyes, and he ran his hand through them to push them back. "I think that if we could just get past our differences–"

"Robert, you didn't let me finish," Melody interrupted, the small flecks of green in her eyes came to the surface.

"Melody...please...don't," Ashley held her friend's hand and gave a slight squeeze to indicate not to go any further.

"Yes, Melody, what more do you have to say?" Patrice asked as she squinted at Melody. The recent treatment of botox did its job, as no line of her forehead was shown.

"I only wanted to say sorry that you're not my father," she belted out defiantly.

Patrice's eyes grew larger, and the botox could no longer contain the wrinkles on her face. Melody knew that her mom wanted to blow a fuse.

"Melody! How dare you, and after all he's done to be nice to you."

"Oh, Patrice, it's quite alright. She is only a teenager and doesn't know better. Just give her some time." Robert's voice oozed with a charm that made Melody's skin crawl. Melody looked up as he locked eyes with her, "I got all the time in the world."

In the backseat, Ashley looked at Melody with sad, Bambi-esque blue eyes. "Melody, do you really have to get into it right now? You know how anxious it makes me...," she picked at her nails one by one.

"You tell me one nice thing he's ever done for me, and then I'll never say anything mean to him again," Melody whispered.

"Well...um..I don't know, I guess marrying your mom was pretty nice, in a way..."

"Yea, I guess it does get her off my back about the debutante thing she normally bothers me about. But he's got no right being labeled as my father. Let's just agree to disagree." Melody's nosed flared slightly at ever calling him "father"

Melody thought about her real father. They had an impenetrable bond, and Dad made sure to instill curiosity and confidence in her. He taught her to not be scared of anything, because even monsters turn out to be people in masks. Sometimes they are hiding behind masks on purpose and others due to unseen mental illnesses. Melody loved when she would go with him to the market four blocks from their New York penthouse. That's where she met so many people that her mother would deem unworthy to talk to, and was able to see firsthand not all get to live a life as privileged as hers. In those days, she gained experience and knowledge that allowed her to excel past what wealth had to offer her–thanks to her dad. Now he wasn't here to live through these experiences with her, but Ashley was and she made sure to keep Melody grounded.

The sense of normalcy that Ashley provided was an important facet of their friendship. Ashley taught her to be more than a rich kid, and Melody repaid by helping Ashley with anything she needed–monetarily or not. Together they became sisters without blood, and never left each other's side.

"Are we almost there?" Ashley whispered.

"Yea, not too far. We still have to go dow...," Melody's voice trailed off as she turned to see them pulling into the gates of the manor.

"Oh my...god...you didn't tell me you guys had...you didn't tell me it was *this* big!"

The Rolls Royce pulled onto the road to the manor. On both sides there stood a row of large weeping willows that stood high enough to create a cast over the pathway. Directly in front of them was the manor itself. It was made of gray stones, and when looked at from the front one could only see two wings, but hidden inside the square fortress were two more wings to be explored. The home was well-maintained while they were gone, but the ivy had curled itself to the window frames and the trellis that led to Melody's room.

Ashley marveled at the large doorway that seemed to be about 15 feet tall. Her eyes slowly made their way down the marbled stairs, and when she tried to take it all in her brain felt fuzzy. Ashley felt small in comparison to the building, but in reality, she felt small inside. She didn't feel as though she belonged here, at the manor, or with Melody. Her family could never afford this, and her mind exploded at the idea that she'd be there all summer. Her anxiety set in and reeled her back to reality. *I better not break anything, or it'll be my head on a platter*, she thought to herself.

Her big round blue eyes glimmered in amazement, and her glasses slipped down her face.

"Here, let me help you with that". Melody placed her finger in the middle and pushed up.

"I hope there's a library in there", whispered Ashley

"It's in there somewhere, nerd," replied Melody

"Just because she enjoys novels, doesn't make her a nerd, Melody," Robert's voice echoed out, and she hated every word he spoke. *That* voice. It was a voice that ruined their family. The man that wooed and won her mother over two months after her father's death. In recent years, Melody looked back at how things played out. She soon came to the realization that Patrice couldn't have rekindled a relationship with him after her husband's death, but before. Melody wanted nothing to do with him, but here they were in the same car, and now she has to call him her *ugggh...stepfather*.

Chapter Two

The black car stopped in front of the manor, and a butler came out to greet them. He was dressed in his best black suit, and he came around and grabbed the bags, placing them on a trolley.

The butler then made his way to the front of the car to allow Patrice to exit the vehicle. Her long, slender legs were accentuated by her black heels as they stood upon the stone of the driveway. She shimmied her skintight dress down to its appropriate length and stayed put until Robert came around to escort her inside.

When they were at the top of the stairs, the butler came around to Melody's door.

"Ah, hello there Mrs. Melody! I hope you remember me." His eyes smiled when he talked to her, and she instantly remembered him and gave him a hug.

"Of course, I remember you Bernie!" Melody let go and fist-bumped him, which led to a secret handshake that Ashley had never seen Melody do before. "How could I forget you? You were the only one who had enough time to play *Find the Killer* with me as a child."

Bernie chuckled, "Oh, yes Ms. Melody. You were definitely a different kind of child. I never quite understood your game, but knew you'd find the culprit no matter what." He waved his hand beckoning them to follow as he led them into the foyer of the house. Its gray stonework did not allow for a cheery entrance.

Ashley touched one of two white pillars holding up the outside as she walked in. "*Find the Killer*? Geez, Melody, what kind of games were you playing as a child?"

"Oh, just the normal ones where I solve a crime. Didn't you play games like that?" Melody genuinely asked.

"No! The closest to it was Bloody Mary. That game scared the crap out of me just saying the name. I never wanted to see if it were true. I just wanted to seem cool. Never did I ever play a game about a killer!" Ashley said, placing her hand on her heart.

"There weren't actually killers. What do you take me for? Some kind of psycho?"

"Well..."

"No! Bernie would take my favorite episodes off of shows like *48 Hours*, and make the house into a crime scene. Then I'd deduce who could or couldn't be the killer based on things like blood patterns, and such." Melody calmly told Ashley, as if it wasn't ridiculous.

"Oh, yea, just your typical everyday eight-year-old playing with blood patterns. Are you sure there's not something seriously wrong with you? You say it as if it's normal."

"That's because it is normal. I don't get the big deal, Ash. It's just a game." They paused at the top of the steps. "Hey, maybe we could play it here sometime!"

Ashley shook her head, knowing that she would be the next victim to be lured into a weird game of *Find the Killer*. Melody was strange, but not strange enough to deter her friendship. Melody brought out the good in Ashley, and kept her from being a social piranha, as her anxiety got the best of her.

Ashley was book smart, and it usually worked in their favor with Melody as the sleuth. Ashley could back up the data of why something was or wasn't probable. In most cases, she provided background information for things that Melody never heard of before. They went together like peanut butter and jelly, or as Melody would say: like peanut butter and bologna.

Melody, not wanting to even be there, threw her bag on the floor to the right, while Ashley's face dropped in awe. Cobwebs were in every corner, with sheets still on major pieces of furniture that lay around. Many pictures lined the walls of the dreary estate that were of the Meltronts of the past.

Melody felt uneasy being there for the first time in so long. She felt as if it was new territory all over again. The last time she was here, it was with her father. This time she was here with strangers to call her parents, and a friend who thought the whole situation was out of a movie. The eyes of the paintings burrowed into her mind, and she felt lightheaded.

"Hey, I'm going to go grab a snack. Do you want anything?"

"No, I'm okay. I just want to look around for a bit." Ashley was tracing her fingers along the hallways of the home. Leaving behind her a trail of dust scattering into the air.

Melody walked to the kitchen where she was greeted by another familiar face, her housemaid Merna. Merna had been her nanny as a child, and Melody looked up to her as a mother figure, since she wasn't close to Patrice. They would laugh and giggle over peanut butter and bologna sandwiches—which was her and her father's favorite sandwich—and joke about the latest party her mother was invited to.

Merna hadn't changed a bit since those times, and the only thing new was the soft wrinkles placed carefully around her eyes distinguishing the years that had passed. "My baby!" her arms open for a hug.

"I missed you too, Merna." Melody hugged her, and with it felt comfort. Merna smelled like home with a slight tinge of cinnamon, and it brought back memories of her father.

"Everything ok, sweetheart?" Merna's brow furrowed with worry.

"Yea, it's fine. It's just," her voice trailed off. "It's just, I feel like when dad died, so did my life. It hasn't been the same, and Patrice still doesn't act like a mother. And now...now I have to deal with *him*."

"I know, honey. Sometimes life, it throws you curveballs. Sometimes it grabs you by force when you least expect it, and it rips your heart out. Life isn't a cakewalk, honey. Life is a journey, and journeys are tough at times."

"I know, Merna." Melody whispered as she lowered her eyes to the floor.

Merna pulled Melody back in for another hug. "I know, baby. Just know that your father would be proud of who you are. I'm proud, and I'll always be here for you when needed."

Melody inhaled the aroma one last time. Her fingers slightly gripped deeper into Merna's back as she didn't want to let go, but also didn't want anybody to see her emotions. "Thanks, Merna, I needed that." She climbed onto a tan stool and sat down at the counter. "Do you think you can make me the special? I need comfort food to help me through."

"Sure, honey. Coming right up!" Melody crumpled onto the counter. Her head buried into her arms, as she struggled to see any positives of this summer.

On the other side of the house, Ashley created a trail attempting to find the library. Her finger slowly pressed on the blue wallpaper that adorned the walls as dust wiped off. She wanted to read anything and everything she could get her hands on this summer. Melody had told her before that there were many books that were first editions or signed by the authors themselves. It was her father's collection, and he loved to read, so presumably, there was a lot.

Ashley walked around the corner and peered into a dark room. Her hand crept before her, as she fumbled for the light switch. The light flickered on into a dim, faded yellow. It was just enough to see the books, but not enough to read them. She looked around at the three walls covered with books. *Jackpot!* Ashley was in heaven. She fingered through the novels. "Thoreau. Hemingway. Orwell. Steinbeck. Woolf. Bronte," she whispered to herself, and with each book, her heart raced faster. "How am I ever going to find the time to finish all of these?" Her hand pulled out the Ray Bradbury on the wall. "I guess I'll start here!" She walked over to the desk that sat in the middle of the room and was about to pull out the chair.

"What do you think you're doing in here?" A booming voice startled her, and she jumped resulting in her dropping the novel.

"Um..I...uh. I'm sorry. I...I thought that Melody said it was ok". Ashley's voice quivered from anxiety, "I...I was just looking at the books." She sheepishly turned her eyes away, not wanting to look at Robert directly.

He slammed his hand down onto the desk in front of her. "I want you and *her* to stay out of this room!" His voice traveled down the hallways, echoing the angry sentiments onto the walls.

Ashley broke down. Tears dripped slowly down her face, as she tried so hard to keep them in. She didn't like to show weakness. Anxiety didn't care and she burst into tears.

Melody ran into the room. "What is going on in here? Why are you yelling at her?"

"I wasn't yelling. I was telling her that this office is off-limits to her and you! This office is going to be locked at all times, and it's my private space. I want you both out of here, now!"

"Come on Ashley, let's go. We wouldn't want to be near his precious office anyway." Ashley stepped forward, afraid to go too close to Robert. She knew he had an anger problem, but had never witnessed it until now. The book was still in her hand from when she picked it up. Not wanting to anger him any further, she proceeded back to their room with it where she placed it on top of her dresser.

"I've never seen him act like that, Mel." The tears trickled out and her breathing slowed. "I didn't even do anything, but go into the room and touch the books."

"I know, Ash. Something's definitely up. I've been trying to figure out what's wrong with him." Melody paced the floor of their large room. Two king-size beds, one on each side, sat in the corners. Ashley noticed that this room had more light in comparison to the office, but that the same putrid green color was plastered on the walls

"Why was there barely any light in there? It was so dim I could barely read." Ashley scrunched her nose, her freckles showing in the sun's rays, "Strange for a library."

"I don't know, I guess old bulbs? This house hasn't been used in eight years. The only people who have come here are Merna and Bernie to maintain the property."

"I guess..." Ashley stretched out on her bed, her face muddled with tears as she placed it into the crooks of her arms facing towards the large window. Melody stood there, looking outside at the darkness that was inching in. A fog was settling from the nearby swamps, and it created an eerie presence around the manor. It caused Ashley's anxiety to increase, but for Melody, it created a feeling to start a good mystery. Melody knew that something was wrong with Robert. He was lying or hiding something. But what was it?

She looked at her reflection in the pane of glass. *You're up to something, and I'm going to figure out what it is.*

Chapter Three

June 21

Dear Diary,

Today was the first day of summer vacation. How exciting is it that I get to spend my summer with Melody in a huge mansion?! It doesn't have a "homey" feeling, but it does have a fancy living feeling.

I feel like I'm going to end up breaking something, and everything is so...*antique*. Mom would have a cow if she had to pay for anything damaged here. It's best if I just keep my hands to myself and only touch what I brought.

I had a strange experience with Melody's stepdad earlier. He yelled at me for being in his office...I was only touching the books, I swear!

Diary, it's going to be a long summer not being able to open up a book from that library. I saw so many books, ones that I love, and ones that I have yet to read.

I hope that Robert changes his mind and lets me at least read the books, but I am sure as not asking. That man scares the daylights out of me. He seems charming around other people, but now I see a darker side to him as Melody spoke of. Maybe it's just his personality. Fingers crossed there's no more awkwardness.

Love,

Nervous Nelly Ash

Chapter Four

That night, Melody lay in her bed and ran through memories of her father in her mind. She wished she could remember him...hug him...if only she had had more time to learn from him, and get to know him. Robert was the devil reincarnated, and she could see through the mask that hid his sinister personality.

Ashley was passed out in the bed across the room. Her snoring made every cell of Melody's hold back from throwing something at her. She hated to hear Ashley snore, and most times wore earplugs. Unfortunately, Melody left her plugs at home and she succumbed to the dreadful sound. She pulled back her blush floral comforter and tiptoed across the wooden floorboards.

CREEEEAAAK!

Melody slowed down and paused before starting again as she crept to Ashley's bedside. Ashley's mouth was agape and drool ran out like a river. Melody raised her pillow up to smother the noise out herself. She began to lower it when she heard another noise. One that she knew could not be her or Ashley. She turned around and listened—each breath grew shallow. *What was that sound?* It sounded like rattling on the old inner brick walls of the manor. Like there was movement throughout; echoing as if the area was more cavernous than it lets on.

Melody placed her ear on the wall of their room. It felt cool, which was strange for the time of the year. Outside appeared foggy, and the cracked window across the room revealed that despite the breeze, the air was warm and musty. *So why a cold wall?*

The sound was still there, reverberating off of whatever room it was coming from, but still appearing to become more distant. Melody ran back over and attempted to wake Ashley up.

"Ash! Ash!" Her voice rang with excitement. Melody didn't know what this mysterious sound was, nor what it could be, but she did know that her only goal for the summer was to solve a mystery. Initially, she believed the mystery would end up being something along the lines of "Oh, who ate the last piece of pie?", or "Where did this dog come from?" She had begun the trip with low expectations, but they were rising and ideas came running through her head. *Could it be a robber? Nah, not in there.* Her mind raced with ideas, and each one made her enjoy it more and more.

"Ash!" She finally shoved her awake. Ashley sat up in her bed still in a daze; her hair matted in the back and wiry in the front from the tossing and turning she did; mixing with the drool she produced with each head-wrenching snore.

"No, I don't want to do your homework—"

"Don't want to do my what?! Ash, have you gone bonkers? Come on, hurry up!"

"What...where..what?" Ashley's brain slowly caught up to her mouth as she attempted to produce words that would string along and make sense.

"Ashley, come on! I hear a noise in the walls, let's go figure out where it's coming from."

"I'm coming mother!"

"Mother?! I'm not your mother! Get up!" Melody pulled on Ashley's arm, but with each heave, Ashley just fell deeper into sleep. "God the woman can sleep, I guess." She dropped Ashley's arm and crossed her arms in a huff as she straightened out her pajama shorts. "I guess, I'll just go by myself."

Melody proceeded to open the large, wooden door and was careful to not make a sound that could wake up her parents. How she would hate to see Robert this late at night. She could faintly hear the rattling in the walls as she cupped her ear against the wall—or maybe it was her imagination at this point. She walked down the hallway toward the center of the manor and looked down the staircase. Her and Ashley's room were at the end of the east wing corridor, with her parent's room on the opposing wall.

The east corridor was to her right, and only featured vacant rooms—except for her mother's sitting room. At the bottom of the stairwell, Robert's office was located to the left down the north wing. The south wing was where the kitchen, dining room, and guest quarters were. It was overwhelmingly spacious for a family of three.

An increasingly empty feeling now replaced the once bustling home where Melody recalled playing hide and seek with her father. She had many warm memories of her father, but almost none with her mother. Her mother did "try her best", which to Patricia meant throwing her money at the situation. If Melody was suspended, money was greasing the palms of those in charge. If Melody had a birthday coming up, she didn't pick gifts that would be loved by Melody, but ones that would *enhance* her beauty as her mother would say. Fancy dresses, makeup, and the best that money could buy.

On the other hand, Dan played games, like Hide and Seek, where he'd count to 100 only to skip numbers, slowly stall, and at times forget counting completely. She'd hide in areas that were small enough for her to squeeze into, and hours of laughter would ensue. All of her favorite memories were buried with her father the day he was put to rest.

Melody stopped and wiped the tear that was traveling down her cheeks. *Keep your eye on the prize*, she thought to herself as she tried to hear the sound, but failed. She looked up to see where the noise had originally brought her—Robert's office. She didn't see any lights on in the office and walked down the corridor to check the other two rooms. The one next to the office was closed. A padlock was placed over a piece of metal as if to hide something. She started to walk to the linen closet across the hallway but stopped in her tracks as she heard a slight noise coming from the locked fortress. She turned around and placed her hand against the door to listen. The sound continued, but this time it was footsteps. Melody's heart pumped blood faster through her chest; her ears rang in suspense. *What's in there that I'm not supposed to know about?* She jiggled the door handle and the sound came to a rest just as a hand came from behind her landing next to her face on the door.

"And just what do you think you're doing?" a fuming face greeted her. His dark brown eyes stared at her and appeared to look through her as if there was no soul in him. Robert's nostrils were flaring, and his teeth showed as he seethed in anger.

Melody smiled, "Oh, hi there, Robert. Nice to see you at this fine hour. I was just—" Melody tried to lighten the situation.

He cut her off, "I thought I told you to never go down this wing."

"No, your highness, you told me not to touch your office, remember?" Her smart attitude pressed on his last nerve.

“Don’t come near this corridor or any room in this corridor. Don’t think about them, don’t touch them, don’t enter them.” He demanded this from Melody, who was at her wit's end dealing with the incredulous man.

“Oh, I’m sorry, yes sir!” She put her hand to her forehead and saluted. "I won’t touch your precious office and hiding spot.” Melody turned to walk back to her room. She could feel his eyes burning through the back of her skull as he glared.

Once she was back in her room, she pulled her notepad out of the nightstand and wrote down her thoughts before falling asleep.

Chapter Five

June 22

New Break In The Case:

Mysterious room padlocked

- Robert acting strange about the room and office

Prime Suspect:

- Robert...duh!---But how?

Thoughts:

- Secret wife?
- Robber?---Unlikely
- Could it just be an animal in the walls?

MM

Chapter Six

The sun shone into the open bay windows, and Melody peered out from under her blankets. Ashley was in the crook of the window.

That wasn't there last night, Melody thought. "Ash, what is this?" Melody asked as she pointed to the window now covered in bright blankets and pillows as a seating area.

"Oh, it's just something I put together real fast." Her melodious voice was one that could be representative of a Disney princess. You know the kind that encaptures birds in her radiating tone; mimicking a siren. "You know your room is not inviting. Maybe to a spider, but definitely not another human."

Melody shuddered from the less desirous thoughts of Disney and *princesses* and thought about how dark her room was. "It's not *that* bad. It's not like it's all black or ruffles, or something."

"Oh, it's something. Something straight out of *48 Hours*. Mel, this looks like one of the rooms of a serial killer—no joy anywhere." Ashley tossed a beige throw pillow out of the corner of the beige window sill. "Where's your color? Where's the room of a normal person"

"Look, you know I'm not normal Ash. I'm in love with Dexter for God's sake. I'm not *a* serial killer. I'm in love with *the* serial killer."

"Yea, and apparently your choice of guys has rubbed off onto every other facet of your life. And I thought I was the weirdo," Ashley scoffed as she flopped onto the bed.

KNOCK, KNOCK!

The girls looked over to see Bernie standing there; a smile on his face as he motioned towards the kitchen downstairs. "On your feet, young ladies! Breakfast is done. Merna cooked up a storm for your first breakfast back."

"Oooo, I hope there's bacon!" Ashley shoved Melody out of the way, and down the spiral case, she went; disappearing around the corner with her ponytail chasing after her.

"I think someone's excited," Bernie chuckled.

"Bernie, I think that's an understatement." Melody rolled her eyes and proceeded to follow Bernie into the dining room where breakfast was being served by Merna.

Robert and Patrice were at separate ends of the long wooden table. Held together decoratively with fresh roses and daisies from the garden. The aroma seemed to stave off the smell of must that emitted from the walls. Melody likened it to mothballs in an elderly care home. Ashley claimed it was mildew, something she read in a book somewhere. Either way, it was not a pleasant odor.

In the center, at each side were two chairs—one for each girl—and an adult at each end. None of them were closer than five feet from the other, and the distance felt stifling.

"Darling, have you read the third page yet? It seems that young girl you worked with is still missing," the paper shuffled in Patrice's hands.

"No, love, I'm still in the economy section. It seems that the housing market is booming. Perhaps, we should sell the beach house, and rebuy something new when the market slows again." He pushed off the underlying inquisition that Patrice was trying to get out of the story.

"Robert..." The paper lowered, and Patrice's ice-cold glare peeked out above; daggers pointed directly at the man of the table, and he muttered to himself as he stood up..

"God damn it, Patrice! I wish you'd stop bringing her up! I fired her months ago because that's what you wanted! What more am I supposed to care?" he stormed out of the room, and once more the paper rose back up as Patrice turned the page.

Not one to understand the silence, or wait an appropriate amount of time before action, Melody spoke as soon as the door slammed him from behind. "Mom, did you happen to hear anything strange last night?"

"Strange?" Patrice attempted to look concerned, but the botox in her forehead didn't allow her.

"Yea, I heard something that sounded like a rattling in the wall. It definitely wasn't an animal, and I followed it to Robert's office...""Robert's office?" she shrieked. "You know that his office is off limits!"

"I know, but the sound...I followed it there, and..."

Patrice cut her off once more, "You're probably just imagining things. Guilty consciousness makes you do that, and you know never to go near there."

"Yea, but, Robert was there..."

"Yea, honey, do whatever you want, just stay away from his office. I know I don't need the headache of listening to him complain about you more." Her freshly manicured hand rubbed her temple, "God, you are giving me gray hairs well before my day!" And with that, Patrice, too, left the room in a huff.

Ashley took her fork and prodded at the food anxiously, before she looked to Melody, "...at least there was bacon." She averted her eyes and began to eat once again. Melody knew that her eating was a coping mechanism for her anxiety. And anxiety ran rampant around the Meltronts. Patrice, herself, was currently on a healthy diet of Xanax, which allowed her to maintain an aloof personality in public. This kept her from pulling her hair out at her husband's indiscretions. The downfall was that this diet didn't allow for much room to add in alcohol, which Patrice also loved. Every morning around ten—except for days that included publicity stunts—Patrice would drink several chardonnays to get the day rolling. Flouncing around the house in a stupor that Melody was used to, but Ashley was afraid of.

Ashley's father was an alcoholic as well, but not one like Patrice—he was an angry drunk, which would explain why he was in jail. Her father had come close to killing her mother and was sent away. Ashley refused to ever talk about it, but Melody pieced it together throughout their years of friendship. And as the summer would go on, Melody knew she would see the depletion of snacks, as Ashley survived a summer of Patrice and Robert.

"Did you hear anything last night? I mean, over your incessant snoring?"

"Hmmm? Sound?" Scrambled eggs filled her mouth as she spoke through them. "I don't think so. I don't really remember last night too much. This place kinda overwhelms me."

"That's weird...there was definitely something in the walls. I heard it go from our room to Robert's office."

"Mel, how could it move from room to room?"

"I don't know, but I want to find out. Let's sneak into his office sometime this week, and snoop."

"Snoop? I don't know, Mel. He's pretty adamant about you not going in there. I think we should just leave it be. I don't really want to upset them."

"Oh stop, he's not going to know. We'll plan it out, and go in when we know he's not going to be there. There's something in there that he's hiding, Ash. And I intend to find out what it is, even if he grounds me or some stupid crap."

"You're not going to stop are you?"

"Of course not," Melody picked up her fork and stabbed her over easy eggs, and watched as the yolk slowly drizzled out and over the rest of the contents of her plate. *If only this egg was Robert.*

Chapter Seven

June 24

Dear Diary,

Day #15 at Mel's mansion. And what a weird time. How do people live like this? Such extravagance and waste, and for what? A decrepit home. There's no color...at all. No warmth like at mom's (especially when she bakes her wonderful snickerdoodle cookies). This house is like her parents: rigid and cold.

The atmosphere reminds me of when dad used to drink all the time and come home yelling at mom. It saddens me to think that Melody lives like this too. I try not to be seen around her parents; blending like a chameleon. Robert...he scares me. Mel hates him, and obviously, I have to as well on that end, but there's actually something up with him. I don't trust his intentions. I also don't know what he's hiding, but it's something, and Mel's going to be the hound that snooped too far—I know it. I guess she's going to drag me down with her, and that makes my anxiety flare. But, hey....what are best friends for?

Sincerely,

Anxious Peanut Butter

Chapter Eight

A few nights later, the girls quietly ate their meals and excused themselves to bed. They waited until they heard the door to Patricia's and Robert's room close—after hours of hearing them drink and argue in the foyer—and then they got out of their beds. The two of them crept down the hall and tiptoed down the staircase to get to Robert's office. They came up to the door, and Mel slowly attempted to turn the knob.

"Of course, it's locked..." Melody said as she pulled a skeleton key from her pants pocket, Melody pushed it into the lock and twisted it as she pushed the door open.

"Where did that key come from?" Ashley asked.

"Oh, this thing? It was my dad's, I'd always put it somewhere only he and I could get to at the end of each summer. This time it was taped to the bottom of my bed."

"What *normal* person has a skeleton key, and just says 'Oh, this old thing? It's nothing'." She shook her head and entered the office as she followed along with Mel's plan.

"Because it is nothing. It's just a key. Only this time it's being used to help us solve a mystery...so I guess it does give it a hint of cool." Melody walked to the desk, as Ashley meandered towards the books. "I'll start looking here, and you tell me if you find anything strange or of interest along the walls.""Sounds good." Ashley fingered the spine of each novel that she passed. Each one made her heart skip a beat...Hemingway, Poe, Hawthorne...*they're all here.* After they searched for thirty minutes, Ashley's eyes turned from the last shelf on the left side of the office, when she noticed something. There were several books with different bindings than the rest, and all with names she'd never heard of. Her eyes widened with horror, as she realized just what the books had written inside of them.

"Um...Mel...I think you'll want to come see this." Her voice wavered with a new emotion; one that made her unsure of how to feel. Was she in fight or flight mode? She wasn't sure. But what she did know for sure now was that Robert was definitely hiding something. And it might be more sinister than either of them had expected.

"Woah. What the hell is all of this?" The book titles made Melody's stomach turn: *How to Tie Knots* and *Anthology of Serial Killers*. There were books on soundproofing rooms and ones about whipping people into submission. The hair on their necks stood on end. Ashley's was from the increasing anxiety that plagued her, but Melody's was because she knew she was finally onto something.

"Mel, look at this weird one over here!" Ashley now stood at the back shelves. "Here, it's dusty, but definitely in the same realm as the others over there."

Melody maneuvered the book from her left to right hand as she turned it over. She pushed her lips together and blew off the dust that was layered thick. Under the final layer, were four letters written in silver lettering on the brown leatherbound book: *M A R A*.

"Who's Mara?"

"She's Robert's teaching assistant at the university. Or I mean, *was* the teaching assistant. He fired her about two years ago. Mom made him or something, I don't remember everything, but it was a whole to do." Her eyebrows furrowed together. "I just don't understand why he'd have a book with her name on it in his office."

"Well, go on, open it up!" Ashley said. She was excited but nervous to discover the contents.

Melody opened to a random page. It contained pictures pasted on its white pages. All were on a polaroid camera and appeared to show an affair between Robert and Mara. The photos near the top showed them kissing in the car, and Melody rolled her eyes at his bottom-level indiscretions. She looked further down the page as the pictures got worse and worse. They looked as though a person was hiding while the pictures were taken. The leaves were seen in the corners as the couple walked into a hotel room.

Ashley glanced at the pictures at the bottom taken by someone as they peered through the glass while the couple fornicated in the back seat of the Rolls Royce. "Ewww! We sat there!" exclaimed Ashley.

"Shhh." Melody put her finger to her lip and continued to flip through the pages. The pictures created a timeline that Melody had known nothing about. The odd part was that they were all taken by someone else.

CLICK, CLICK, CLICK.

The girls heard the distinct sound of Robert's black shoes each time they hit the wooden floors. Ashley panicked, "What do we do? What do we do?" Her arms flailed in front of her face before she placed a hand on each temple as she tried to focus on what they were doing.

"Come this way. Hurry!" Melody beckoned her to the corner of the room, where a large vent was placed behind a palm-like plant. She slipped the register off and had Ashley go in first. Melody followed behind and slowly pulled the register back into place right as Robert entered.

He pushed the light on in the room and looked around. "That's strange, I thought I locked this..." His voice seemed skeptical. Almost like he could tell the girls had been in there. They stayed still in the vent and held their breath as he glared around the room.

Melody's finger pressed against her lips. Ashley was shaking but knew not to make a sound and expose themselves.

Robert didn't seem like he knew they were still in there, just that they *were* there at some point. He shuffled the documents on his desk, when Melody opened up the book one more time. Inside she found newspaper clippings. Several were from two years ago. These ones conveyed Robert's arrest—arrested twice for domestic abuse and assault against Mara. *This is why things changed around then. No wonder mom didn't want Mara around the office. She knew that he was cheating. She knew and still stayed.*

Melody flipped some more towards the back. This time the newspaper clippings weren't about Robert; instead, they featured Mara as the headline: "Teaching Assistant Missing" and "Local Professor Cleared of Wrongdoing in TA's Death". Each one was about Mara; each one claimed that Mara was missing since last winter...Last winter, when Robert went missing for long periods of time, and when the arguing started again between Patrice and him.

The girls looked on until Robert finally grabbed what he was looking for and left. He took one more look behind him and flipped off the light.

They exited the vent, Melody ran to the doorway to make sure Robert was definitely gone.

"That was so close. Mel, I don't think we should keep going. Sometimes things are better left unknown, and maybe this is one of those things."

"Ash, you know I can't do that. He's up to something, and I'm going to figure out what it was. We already know that they were having an affair, that he fired her, and sometime after she went missing. I think it's a perfect way of seeing that he's the devil I've always known him to be."

"Yea, he's obviously demented, but Mel, what if he catches us? What if he does something to keep us quiet? What if–"

"Stop! I don't care about the *what-ifs*, I care about the what, why, and how. What did he do; why did he do it; how did he do it? I'm going to catch him, Ash. I'm going to expose him to the world for what he really is."

Ashley accepted the situation for what it was. Melody was determined, and she was going to have to back her up. They tiptoed back upstairs, and slowly closed their door.

Across the hallway, they listened as Robert muttered to himself. He realized he had left the office unlocked, and the girls heard as he walked downstairs to place the lock back on. They closed their eyes as his footsteps grew louder until he was in his room That night neither got sleep, as all sorts of thoughts raced through their minds.

Chapter Nine

June 29th

Notes:

Ashley and I need to figure out if Robert had anything to do with Mara's disappearance. Did Mom know about the affair and have them trailed? Why are those books in the office about soundproofing walls? Is there someone in that room? So many questions, but all paths lead back to Robert...interesting.

New Break in Case:

- Room next to Robert's office has a padlock...why?
- Robert has strange books in office relating to kidnapping and murder
- What happened to Mara?

Need to find that key! One last try in the office

MM

Chapter Ten

June was coming to its close, and the rising temperatures reminded everyone it was the peak of summer. The girls grew more and more determined as the days passed to solve the mystery—much to Ashley's chagrin—and they molded their sleep routines to the slow hustle of summer. Every night they stayed up late to work out how to find more clues or see the nighttime patterns of Patrice and Robert. This meant a late start to each morning, and the second to last day of June didn't look any different.

Bright rays of sunshine crept in between the cracks of the curtains and touched Melody's eyes. Her eyes fluttered open and she squinted at the sun for waking her up at nearly 11 am. She stretched her arms and cracked her neck before waking up Ashley.

July 4th was the upcoming weekend, and that meant that the Meltronts would be having their annual Fourth of July Event. It was one of only two days during the summer that couldn't be redone without a big to do. And much to Robert's discontent about holding the parties at the manor, Patrice insisted. And when Patrice insisted, it meant it was happening with or without him.

"Ugh, parties," Melody despised parties. She hated people, and would rather chop off her right arm than attend them. But each time she was forced to partake in them and wear the demeaning outfit her mother would pick out for her.

Today was different, though...today no outfit was picked out, and Patrice was too busy while she yelled around the house drunk in the morning, on glasses of chardonnay.

Melody moaned, "This wouldn't be happening if Dad was still alive."

Ashley sat there in her window seat, while she held a fuzzy, blue, square pillow against her chest, and lowered her chin to the top. She could hear the melancholy in Melody's voice as if she was holding back crying, but attempting to hold it together.

Melody was always one to not care, and sound somber and dreary, but this was different. "Mel...are you okay?" Ashley paused for a second, to allow Melody to answer. She began again. "I know you don't talk much about your Dad, but you know you can always tell me anything."

"I know, it's just..." her eyes welled up. "It's just when Dad was around, we didn't do the parties, mom would go by herself, and Dad and I would just play games, or he'd tell me stories. Mom only cares about herself—she never loved Dad. This was his house, not hers. And now it's *theirs*. It's just not the same without him...," Melody said as a tear rolled down her cheek. She brushed it off and pulled her knees up to rest her chin.

"I just want to say I'm here when you need me, and I can give you time if you'd like." She placed her hand on Melody's shoulder and gently kissed her forehead. "I'll be in the garden when you'd like to talk." Her smile was only slight, as she walked out the door.

Melody flopped onto her bed, sobbing into her pillow—a rare sign that she had emotions other than morbid ones. The tears ran down her face, as she looked at the picture of her Dad on the table next to her. "Why couldn't *she* have died instead of you? Why'd you leave me with her?"

Melody reminisced about the last time they spoke before he fell ill.

Eight-year-old Melody rounded the corner of the golden banister, and down the west wing.

"Daddy, you can't catch me!" Her giggles filled the airways.

Fast behind her chased Dan Meltront and his windswept brown hair fell in his eyes. "Melody!" He called out as he turned from wing to wing to decide which one to take. "Come out, come out, wherever you are," a smile crept across his face.

"You can't find me, daddy!" Melody called out from her hiding spot.

Melody hid quietly in the vent register of her father's office.

"Oh, Melody...," his voice rang out. Melody watched as he stuck his head in the room and then heard him walk to the room next door. "Are you...," he paused, "...in there?" He opened the door and jumped in fast to catch her.

He walked across the hall to the linen closet. "Aha!" Dan shouted as he thought he found her again. "Hmmmm."

Melody snickered softly.

"Where could my little girl be?" Dan pondered, "Maybe she's off solving a murder. No, not today, that's for the weekends."

From a distance, Melody heard Patrice's voice, "No more murders in this house," she shouted. "I will not have her grow up being one of those weird children." Away her heels clacked against the floor of the kitchen.

Melody narrowed her eyes.

"It's better than your drinking," Dan muttered lowly so Melody wouldn't hear. Then he remembered he was searching for Melody and his eyes lit up. "If I knew Melody, she wouldn't be hiding in...," Dan trailed off as he ran to the register and lifted it up, "here!"

Dan yanked her out of the spot and gave her a bear hug and kiss on the head.

"You're so silly, daddy! Thought I was playing "Who's the Killer" with Bernie," she slightly bonked him on the head out of affection.

Dan placed her back on the ground and sat at his desk. It was bare, except for the large stack of books he wanted to dig into next. "Come sit with me, sweetheart," he said as he patted his lap.

Melody ran over and climbed up. His blue eyes were soft and caring, and as he entered his mid-thirties, crow's feet were sprinkled about. She placed her hand in his and looked up at him. Her legs swayed in the air. "What is it, daddy?"

"I want you to know that no matter what, I really love you. You know that right?" Dan snuggled her close.

"Of course, I do."

"And you should alwa—"

"Always know both sides of a story before I decide. Blah, blah, blah." Melody mocked.

Dan chuckled, "Yes, that's right." He sat them back in his oversized chair and told her all about the plans they were doing at his charity organization. How they were going to build apartments for the homeless.

Then his tone was more serious. The shine in his eyes disappeared and he looked at Melody. "I want you to know that you can be anything you want to be in this life. Don't chase money."

"I want to be a detective," Melody said as she pretended to look through a magnifying glass.

Dan's expression softened, "That's my girl. Never let mom talk you out of your dreams."

Melody pursed her lips and scrunched her nose. Tiny freckles peppered her nose. "Oh, she won't. I want to help people like you do!"

"I have no doubt you'll always catch the bad guy, Mel-Bel," he ran his fingers through her hair and rocked her in his lap.

Dan grabbed a book from his stack and opened it up: "It was a bright cold day in April, and the clocks were striking thirteen."

They sat in the chair and Dan read Orwell to her until she fell asleep.

Chapter Eleven

June 29th

Dear Diary,

I feel like the walls have eyes. At night time I stare at the fireplace and hear a breeze drifting through the cracks. Melody and I talk in our room to steer clear of Robert and Patrice hearing, but I swear that somehow someone knows what we're discussing.

I prefer the quaint space of my home with mom. It's small enough that I don't think someone could have a place to hide, but it's big enough to fit everything we need. Just right, in my opinion.

These big houses with their large empty rooms. For what? I'll never understand.

The biggest question I have, though, is why do they insist on lining the walkway halls with pictures of old, while men that served in a war? I know, I know. It's their *relatives*, but the thing is...they've never met any of them. Their only connection is the manor.

I do wish they would see that these portraits are nothing more than a creepy idea. Is there a contest out there, somewhere, that asks for people to show off how closely your relatives look like Colonel Sanders? I hope not, at least.

Their eyes stand me down, unlike their ability to stand down the North in the war.

Love,

Ashley

Chapter Twelve

An hour later, Melody woke up from a nap. She had cried herself to sleep thinking about her father. *I wish he were still here.*

Melody recomposed herself and walked to the garden that was filled with dahlias and roses. The smell emitted into the pathway and Melody breathed in deeply to relax.

Ashley sat in the corner, near the old guest cottage on the property. A large wooden swing, with its back towards the woods. Ashley's hair swayed in the wind, as she rocked her feet back and forth; the swing mimicked her movements beneath her and pulled her higher and higher into the air.

Melody waited until she noticed her, and slowed it down. Then she sat quietly next to Ashley—both looked forward as they rocked. "Would you like to talk about it?" Ashley asked as she held out a hand.

Melody grabbed her hand and squeezed. "I just want to sit here, if that's okay."

And so it was as they rocked for ten minutes until Ashley broke the silence.

"Do you remember when we first met in second grade?"

"Of course I do, why?"

"I remember you walking in on that first day of school. You were wearing this atrocious, unmatched outfit. Do you remember it?"

Melody chuckled at the image in her head.

Ashley continued, "It was a bright pink cheetah print top, with a slightly different shade of pink on the leggings. Except, they weren't just plain pink pants or even cheetah prints to match. Oh no—"

Both girls smiled at each other, "...they were zebras!"

The two cracked up over the memory.

"Yea, I remember that outfit, I made sure to never wear it again," Melody rolled her eyes.

"But the thing is Mel, I came to find out that you didn't do that. Your dad chose that outfit. You wore it because you loved him, and you said that you didn't want to upset him," she picked at her fingernails.

"Dad never did have a fashion sense," Melody laughed.

"That was the moment that I knew I wanted to be your friend. You cared about people. I honestly didn't even know you were loaded until I came to your house. And still believed you had to be the child of a worker there. That was until my mom ended up becoming your housekeeper—Then I *knew* you *were* loaded."

Melody smirked at that, "You know money means nothing to me."

"That's because your dad instilled that into you. You never once treated me like someone who was below you because I had no money, and was the daughter of the help. I'm glad that I got to know the *real* you."

"Ash, have you gone bonkers? Are you dying on me or something?" Melody put her hand to Ashley's temple as she pretended to feel for a fever.

"No, I just want you to know that I know your dad meant everything to you, because you act and do the same as he did. I remember those years with you, Mel. I just wanted to remind you that you can still join me at college in Pennsylvania in the fall. It might not be an Ivy League like Harvard or anything, but I can't imagine leaving you behind to deal with them. We can get our own dorm together, and decorate it, however. You can forge your own life, just like your dad."

Melody teared up again. "I love you, Ash, you might be a goon, but you're the best, best friend I could ask for. I wish you could just come to Harvard with me...Mom said I couldn't get Dad's inheritance without going to school."

"Ehh, who needs money when you have me?" Ashley said jokingly as she nudged Melody.

The two sat in silence for a while as they looked at the birds flocking in the sky. Crows cawed as they passed overhead, and a plane soared in the distance. *I wish I could fly away*, Melody thought.

"Ash...," Melody said before she looked at her folded hands, "if I can find out what he's hiding, it might make Mom not care about the stipulations anymore. She'd be too focused on the fallout to remember. We have to go back to his office, and find that key.""But we already looked there."

"It's the only place where he'd hide something of importance. It has to be there."

"Well, you know I'd follow you no matter what. Someone has to be the brains of this. I can't let you go in without facts and statistics. And statistics right now are saying that we have a slim chance of finding that key, Mel."

"All right, it's settled, we're going to find it tonight!" She said as she smiled and jumped up from the swing.

"I mean, that's not what I said...but who cares what Ash says right?! Lol."

"Let's go get this thing going, while they're in town getting supplies. We'll have a solid hour to look," Melody grabbed Ashley's hand and they sprinted to the office to look for the key to the forbidden room once more.

The girls searched every nook and cranny of the office for only thirty minutes, but what seemed like hours. "Mel, I don't think we're going to find this key. He probably has it on him." She wiped her forehead with the back of her sleeve, and her glasses fell down her face.

"I *need* to find out what he's hiding! Keep looking."

Ashley reluctantly went back to searching the cabinets throughout the room, and the other wall of shelves. Melody went tediously through each drawer as she opened it, she hoped that the key was taped somewhere underneath. To her dismay, nothing was there. She started to give up until she glanced at the top of his desk.

In the spot that Robert rustled in the previous night, was a large manilla envelope. It had no writing on it and didn't fit with the rest of his paperwork. Melody slowly lifted it up and opened it. Inside were packets of paper. She pulled out the first one and noticed that it was a police report. It showed that Robert was arrested for domestic abuse, and going against a restraining order for Ms. Mara Lizinski.

"Ash, I think I found something!"

"What is that?" Ashley asked as she jogged over to the desk.

"I think it's Robert's arrest. This one shows that he violated a restraining order that Mara had on him."

"What else is in there? What's this?" Ashley pulled out several polaroid pictures, the same as the ones in the book titled *MARA*. 'Hey, there's writing on this one." She flipped it over to reveal that on the back someone had written:

Robert Meltront and mistress Mara Lizinski at Rochester Motel.

A paper fell out of the envelope, Melody picked it up. "It's a contract. It looks like my mom hired someone to catch the two in the act. These must be the pictures he took."

"I wonder why Robert has them then?"

"Wait, there's more. There are court documents in here. Mom paid his bail on his arrest, and others are from our family attorney. It shows that mom agreed to use a chunk of her inheritance to cover up the affair and arrest."

"She knew about it, and stayed?"

"...I...I can't believe this. She stayed with him, even though he was going behind her back. He's scum. He's not even worth covering up for!" Melody's anger increased each second she thought about it. "Surely, it would have been enough to get a divorce and still maintain the inheritance, without any money going to him! He had an affair and was arrested, and now that girl's missing!"

"Mel, calm down!" Ashley attempted to hold her arms as Melody frantically talked around the room. "Mel! Stop, he can't know we are here!"

The envelope dropped from Melody's hands and onto the floor; the contents spilled out, and Melody fell back into a bust of Plato that sat upon a silver pedestal. When she rushed to grab the falling bust, she realized that it never fell. Instead, the entire bust and pedestal tilted sideways off of the floor, and one wall of the room opened by two inches. The girls ran to see what was inside, and noticed that it wasn't just another room they had stumbled upon, but instead a passageway.

They looked into the crevice. "Melody, this is pretty creepy..." Her voice trailed off as her anxiety once again took over.

"It's fine. I think. I mean, I believe this is the servants' passage. They used to use it back in the day so that servants could get to each room faster. You know because my family couldn't get up to get a drink on their own." The remark made Ashley giggle, and it loosened her anxiety as she calmed down.

"Well that makes sense, I remember reading about this in a couple of stories. But I remember that some of them contained things like a chamber or something that people were locked in.""Oh, you goon, you worry too much!"

At that moment, they both heard the front door open and shut.

"Girls! We're home! Come look at all of the decorations we got!" Patricia rang out.

The panic set in as they rushed to get the passageway shut again. Ashley pulled the pedestal back down and the door slid shut.

Melody noticed again that she dropped the envelope and its contents on the floor. She began to put the documents back inside the envelope when she noticed a packet that had her dad's name on it; about a foot away lay a small, clear, cylinder vial. Melody knew that time was not her friend, so she pulled out her phone and quickly took a video of the vial and the document page by page. She put everything back in, and gingerly placed it back where she found it.

Together, they both shut, and locked the door to the office, just to get to the bottom of their stairs when Robert popped in.

"Hi girls," his voice echoed in Melody's ears. She hated that voice. It sounded like he thought he was outsmarting her. Getting everything he ever wanted. His eyes glimmered, as his lips slightly turned up into a sly smile.

"Hi Robert," Melody sneered.

"Oh, now, come on. How many times do I have to tell you to call me Dad?"

"I'd never call you something as respectable and honorable as that." Melody looked back at Ashley and grabbed her hand. "Come on Ash, let's go get a snack." She led her towards the kitchen and left Robert behind to look at them as they walked away.

"I hope you two weren't in anything you don't belong."

"Mel, he knows," Ashley whispered. Her eyes grew with fear.

"He doesn't know his ass from a hole in the ground."

They walked into the kitchen to be greeted by Patrice.

"Oh, hey girls! How do you like my decorations? I figured Bernie could start putting them up. The caterers will be here Friday to start getting everything together, and the coordinator will be here tomorrow to start doing the outside. I hope you two are ready." Her eyebrows raised as if to show that what she really hoped for was that the girls would be stylish and behaved.

"Yes, Patrice, we have everything we need. I'm taking Ashley later to town to grab some shoes."

"Oh, good. Honey, while you're out make sure to grab whatever you need, as well. Here, take my card." She slid the plastic card on the counter towards Melody.

"Thanks." The two walked out the front door and started the journey toward town three miles away.

Chapter Thirteen

Outside the home, the girls trekked the long driveway. Ashley looked around and stared at the shadows of each tree that she passed. They were so tall that they looked like giants. Their volume filled with each green leaf that was layered between the trees. Their tips reached outward as if to know they were not alone. They stood erect, patiently, in silence.

Ashley shuffled along in the heat, wearing her denim shorts, with a white tank top. She had a light, sheer blue dress shirt over top, and her hair braided to wrap over her shoulder. Fiddling with the end, she looked over at Melody. As always she wore pants. Melody would never be caught dead in a dress "for fun". And she hated the feeling of shorts, stating *they ride up her ass*. She paired it with a striped dress shirt and a black fedora. Melody never dressed normally, and frankly, you could only tell she was still young by her shoe choice. Her pair of black flip-flops clacked with each step.

To Ashley, she reminded her of what you'd expect to see an overworked, balding detective look like in those 80s movies. Like they never married and were bound to the profession.

Soon enough, they hit the gravel, and Ashley broke the ice first. "Mel. Is there a reason we didn't just get someone to drive us out here?" She paused for a minute in conversation and stride, as she picked up her foot and rubbed the heel.

Melody looked stoic, and steady in thought. Ashley knew she took a minute to have everything registered. She hastened her pace to catch back up, and when she did Melody finally realized the question. "I didn't want anybody to hear us."

"Hear us what?"

Melody paused at the side of the road and pulled out her phone. She flipped through the videos and explained what she had seen, and then they went through them again. But this time, it was slower.

"I don't think I quite understand." Ashley quipped.

"Patrice always said that Dad died because of cancer, but according to this, he died of unknown circumstances. I took a video to see if we could find more information in the pages I videoed."

"Do you think your mom had something to do with your dad's death?"

"I wouldn't put it past her, and knowing now what has gone on between her and Robert, I don't think highly of her at this point."

They pressed the buffer button and went through the video frame by frame. Melody paused when she saw the doctor's notes. The details showed Dan had come there complaining of stomach pains and vomiting. During the examination, they couldn't find anything wrong except that his white blood cells were extremely elevated. He threw off all of the classic signs of cancer, along with his blood work seemingly confirming it.

"It states that even though it appeared to be cancer, the head doctor just didn't believe that it's what the issue was, but they had no proof otherwise," Melody said as she clicked off the phone screen.

"Okay, but why do you suspect your mom?"

"Because I found this—" Her voice stopped by an oncoming car. It slowed down until it was right next to them. Inside a young man pushed open the passenger side door.

"Do you two need a lift?" His demeanor was friendly, and his hair was faded with a longer top.

"Sorry! My mom told us not to talk to—-" Ashley was cut off by Melody's hand as she placed it to stop her from talking.

"Why, yes, we'd love a ride. Thank you." They got into the back of the car and closed the door to the black Corolla.

"Hi, I'm Reed." He smiled into the rearview mirror.

"I'm Melody and this is Ashley."

"Nice to meet you. Where are you two headed?" Ashley stared at him each time he looked away. He seemed only a year or two older than them. He had short black hair that was slicked back. His eyes seemed inviting, and not like the typical serial killers that she watched on those shows with Melody.

"Um, we're headed to go shopping in town." Ashley looked up and down still trying not to lock eyes, but she slipped and he noticed—a smirk formed on his face.

"That works great, I'm going there to the bookstore!" His pointer finger raised in the air.

"Bookstore?" Ashley perked up in her seat, and readjusted her posture. "They have one here?

"Haha, do they not usually have one where you're from, or something?"

"I mean, yea...yes. But I just thought that being a small town you wouldn't have that so close." Her eyes glimmered with happiness. *Maybe I can get Melody to read a book!*

"We're not some uncultured swine. We have bookstores," he said as he jokingly rolled his eyes.

"That's not what I meant!" She grew worried that she had caused him to be offended. "I meant—"

"I'm just messing with you," he looked back at her again in the mirror and smiled. His teeth were perfectly straight, and she saw him in a different light. She believed he could be more of a nerd like her. Ashley glanced down at his shirt that featured miniature Tardises from *Doctor Who*. Her inner geek shrieked with excitement.

"Oh," she said as she looked down in embarrassment. "Well, maybe you could show me the bookstore before we shop for a dress. Would that be okay, Mel?"

"Yea, sounds good. Just please stop flirting, I'm not into sappiness, you weirdos."

"Flirting?" Ashley and Reed yelled at the same time. "We're not flirting."

"Okay, you say that. I give you ten minutes before you start talking about some sci-fi show, or old, archaic book that you both relate to. Nerds are like magnets. Go on, don't let me stop you from finding some," she placed her finger in her mouth pretending to gag, "mutual interest."

Ashley sat horrified, but Reed grew quite entertained by the two passengers that joined him for his trip. He looked back at the road, smiled, and drove the final mile to town, not realizing that his life was going to be flipped upside down because of this random chance of meeting.

Chapter Fourteen

The small town buildings popped up quicker than they had disappeared on their arrival. The buildings looked like the ones someone would see in Hallmark movies. A tavern in the center of the town with boutiques placed around it. On the other side was a diner on the corner with large cutout windows at each booth. Ashley liked the homey feel and it made her feel warm and cozy. A large grocery store labeled "Mechers" took up the other end of the strip.

Ashley scanned the street for the bookstore and noticed a quaint rustic building with signage saying "Annie's Books" smack dab between the grocery and diner. Its backdrop was a rural view of the mountains in the distance and large cypresses spread throughout. A person could get lost in the area if they ventured into the unincorporated area.

"Oh, Oh! There it is!" Ashley belted out with excitement before she placed her hand over her mouth. Her eyes grew in embarrassment.

Reed laughed. "Ya know, you are one of the nuttiest girls I've met when it comes to books," his smile made Ashley blush, as she slid her boots against the dusty road. "Here, madam, let me escort you to your destination," he jokingly said as he bowed and allowed her to place her hand in the crook of his elbow.

The three of them made their way to the storefront as Melody trailing behind the duo moved the vial between her fingers. *What is arsphenamine?*

As soon as they entered, a small middle-aged woman greeted them. A silk sixties-style headband wrapped around her wiry graying hair, and under the back tips of her large oval glasses. "Hiya, folks!"

The girls waved back to her as she went on, "Don't get too many people I don't recognize around these parts. I'm Annie, what brings you two girls out in this neck of the woods?" Her welcoming smile drew the girls in.

Melody answered the question before Ashley had to, "My father...I mean my late father," Her small-drawn smile slowly faded back to a sad smirk, "He has a manor down the road, and we're–"

"Oh! The old Meltront Manor? We were all sorry to hear about Dan's passing many years ago. He was definitely loved around here." She placed a hand on Reed's shoulder. "My son here even looked up to him as a hero!"

Ashley leaned in toward Reed. "Is this your mom?"

Reed nodded his head in affirmation with a cheesy grin on his face, "Yup! Why didn't you girls tell me you were coming from that place? We loved your father, he helped my mom get this place up and running when I was just a toddler."

"I don't think I ever really had the chance to know anybody around here. My mom always made sure I was confined to the place. She never wanted me to fraternize with anybody she'd deem *lowly*." Melody's body twitched in anger at all that her mother had denied her over the years in order to maintain the perfect image.

Ashley stepped forward and slowly made a patting motion with her hands, "I mean not that Mrs. Patrice would think *you're* lowly or anything...but she's just...umm, extremely picky on who she talks to," Ashley tried to lighten the mood with a bad attempt to say Patrice would have found them to be bottom of the barrel.

"Oh, don't sweat it, darlin'. I know all about her, and I don't hold anything against you when it comes to her. She's one of those starlets that thinks she can get away with anything." Annie's eyes twinkled in the lights as if her life was carefree. Melody was envious of that look, as her mom pushed everything down her throat. Melody could never be free with Patrice.

"One time, years ago, I remember her berating Mr. Mecher down in the grocery store because he refused to put in credit card machines. Man does he not like your mom. Even has a picture up of her on the wall, stating that she's to be escorted out if she harasses the workers again." Reed raised his eyes to show just how much he also thought Patrice was dramatic.

"Sounds like mom," Melody groaned as she placed a hand on her forehead and pressed her temple.

Her other hand fell upon the vial in her pocket and she had a pivotal break in the mystery. "Wait, before I forget, do you happen to have any books on a drug called "arsphenamine"?"

"Arsphenamine," Annie cupped her chin in her hand, "Why does that word sound so familiar? Here let me look it up and see for ya."

Annie walked to the back room while Ashley began to look around. Reed attentively pointed out his favorite authors, and Ashley showed him her favorite novels. The two seemed like they knew each other for a longer period of time than an hour. It felt lonely for Melody who normally never had competition in the friend department. Ashley and she never made friends besides each other and that's how Melody enjoyed it.

Melody watched as Ashley's face lit up and she was able to talk in the presence of a boy—which meant he wasn't just *some boy*. Maybe he was the jelly that was supposed to be with the peanut butter in their friendship sandwich. A faint smile appeared on Melody's face just as Annie walked back into the room.

"I knew I recognized that word! It's arsenic, love," Annie scrunched her mouth to the left trying to unravel just what a sixteen-year-old girl would be wanting to know about arsenic. "Is there something you're wanting to know about it?"

"I was just wanting to learn more about it. It's for a science class project."

"Class project in the summer?" Annie questioned.

"Oh, you know. Honors courses always try to push to learn on all days of the year—even summer," Melody rolled her eyes as she said it to signal that it was more of a pain in the butt than learning for fun.

"I see. Well, either way, I do have a few books here, I'll grab them while your friend peruses the shelves, and have them ready for ya." Annie smiled as she glanced over to see Reed happily interacting with Ashley.

"Hey, goon, are you ready to go soon? I found what I was looking for."

"Already? But I don't want to look for a dress, I can wear something I already have. Can't we just stay a little longer?"

"Yea! Can't you just stay a little longer?" Reed pushed his lower lip into a pout.

"Yea, Mel, pwetty pwease?" Ashley chimed in pouting her lips too.

"Oh, jeez, I don't need two of you doing this to me. Come on Reed, you can just come with us, I guess."

Annie bagged up all that she had on arsenic and Ashley's new books by Poe and Thoreau. "I also threw in a book that I think you'll love to read as well," her eyes bounced happily between the girls, and when they landed on Reed she gave him a knowing look to be careful.

"Bye Mrs. Annie!" Ashley waved as they stepped out of the front door; the bell jingled above them as the three of them hit the pavement to the boutique across the road.

"So why exactly are you looking up information on arsenic?" Reed asked Melody while he looked both ways for traffic.

"I told you for a science project." Melody briskly walked ahead to avoid the interrogation.

"Oh, duh for a science project, that doesn't sound suspicious and fake. What's the real reason?" He lowered his face and raised his eyes to show he wasn't going to pull a fast one on him.

"It's nothing!" Melody shouted behind her.

Ashley and Reed waited until Melody was almost to the door of the boutique. Her arm reached for the door when they ran at her and playingly fumbled her from the doorway. Ashley looked Melody in the eye, her eyes danced like ocean waves and Melody knew she had to tell.

"Uggh, fine. Here, just promise not to tell anyone," she said as they locked pinkies.

"I promise," Reed agreed as he reached out his pinky.

The pinky promise was solidified.

"I found this vial while we were snooping around my stepfather's office this morning." Melody pulled the vial out of her pocket, "I know he's up to no good, and for some reason, my mom is lying about my father's death. I have to get to the bottom of it."

"Oh, shit! You're living some real-life Hamlet stuff," Ashley looked at Reed. Her heart fluttered at his reference to Shakespeare.

"Ham-what?" Melody asked, confused.

"Don't tell me you don't know what Hamlet is! I mean you're in a similar setting. Your mother remarried quickly after your father's death—to his best friend even! There's now arsenic involved. What more irony do you need?!" He questioned as he shook his hands before him.

Reed quickly pointed out multiple similarities between them, as Melody fell into a trance.

"So in this Ham-thing, the stepfather killed the father, correct?"

Ashley nodded.

I never thought of Robert as the killer, but it would make sense. The two of them did get married not long after Dad's death.

"Mel, what's wrong?" Ashley held her friend's hand and squeezed. "Are you okay?"

Melody looked over at Reed and Ashley as her face turned pale, and her eyes grew sadder at the idea, "What if Robert killed my father?"

Chapter Fifteen

Later that night, Melody still couldn't get the thought of "what if" out of her mind. "Ash..," Melody's voice sounded weak and on the brink of tears. "Ash, are you still awake?"

"Yea, Mel. Want me to come over there?"

"I just can't stop wondering if maybe mom isn't hiding something and really Robert poisoned dad to get him out of the picture. What if.." Melody's voice stopped as the lump in her throat enlarged. She pushed back any emotions she could muster.

Ashley climbed out of her bed and into Melody's. "Mel, I know there are a lot of things running through your head right now, but we can't—".

"Why would mom lie about dad's diagnosis though? Why did the two of them get married so fast?"

Ashley had never seen Melody cry in all of the years of their friendship–except for when Dan died. She didn't know what to do for her friend, so she sat there and held her close while she allowed Melody to cry into her chest. Ashley steadily stroked her hair and kept her ears open for any more venting Melody needed to do.

"Mel. I know this isn't going to be exactly what you want to hear right now, but maybe it's time to stop with this whole vendetta against Robert. We're stuck here with him the whole summer, and we might as well make the best of it. All any of this is going to do is find more reasons for you to hate the man."

"Oh, Ash, but I already hate the man. I hate him with my entire being. I hate him for ruining my family. Dad always told me to call him uncle, but he's not worthy of any title." Melody swung her pillow in frustration, knocking over the bag of books that were on her nightstand. Only one book toppled out labeled *History of Meltront Manor*.

Ashley got down to pick it up, "This must be the surprise Mrs. Annie put in your bag. Seems pretty cool, it has your manor on it, Mel."

"Dad never really told us much about this place. All I know is that he got it after graduating from Yale because he was the only heir for his grandfather's estate–and he never liked talking about that side of the family since his father wanted nothing to do with the man".

"Maybe this book can give you answers about your family, that would be great!" Ashley attempted to look at the bright side of things. "It might even be able to show us how to get into the locked room."

The girls sat there for hours as they scanned the pages of the large hardback. Melody recognized a few faces of aunts and uncles that were long gone, but as they reached the final pages they got the treasure they were looking for.

"Ash, look, you were right! It's a map of this place."

"Let's see...well there's the entrance, the south wing, the north wing, and east and west wings. I don't see where the entrances are for the hidden staircase though." Ashley could barely make out the lettering that was etched over the pictures detailing what the rooms were and their locations. "Wait, I think I see something here," Ashley said excitedly as she brushed away the smudge that hid the chambers: Servant's Quarters. "Well, would ya look at that! It looks like it's not only a passageway but also where they use to house the servants! How wild!"

"That would make sense," Melody squinted at the pages, "I know Dad never liked the idea of separating us from the help and he wanted us to live as equals, maybe they lived there when my grandfather was in charge. We should ask Bernie tomorrow, he will know. He's been with the family for forty years, I believe."

"Forty years? Man, what a life to live stuck in the walls for over twenty years, if it's true." Ashley shuddered in bewilderment.

"You're telling me. I've been locked in mom's walls for sixteen of 'em." The two laughed at the remark before Melody paused. "Ash?"

"Yes, Mel?"

"Promise you'll never leave me like everybody else?" Her eyes teared up at the thought of losing her friend.

"I'll never leave. What kind of bologna sandwich would you be without your peanut butter, silly!" And on that note, they turned out the lights and held each other until they fell asleep.

CREEEEAAAK!

Ashley's eyes fluttered open.

CREAAAKK!

She looked around the room as she stared hard at shadows to make sure they weren't a figure. Nothing there. After waiting a few moments she closed her eyes thinking she had dreamt the sounds.

CREEEEAAAK!

The sound of chains clinking against the walls startled her again. "Mel!" Ashley nudged Melody awake. "Mel! Do you hear that?"

Melody immediately reached into her nightstand and pulled out a flashlight. "Yup! Now let's go slowpoke, we have a mystery to solve."

The two girls slowly crept out of their bedroom and down the hall. The sound would go in and out as they walked the long hall past Patrice and Robert's room and down the stairs.

Melody peaked into the crack of the master bedroom. She placed her finger to her mouth and motioned for Ashley to be silent. Poking her head in, she couldn't see who was still in bed, but she did know that one body was missing. She motioned for Ashley to walk towards the steps.

They leaned over the banister and looked down. The light was glowing from Robert's office, and a shadow danced in the light as if someone was pacing the floor inside.

"It must be Robert down there," Melody whispered. "Let's get closer, and see if the sounds are him."

They each descended the stairs and darted quickly to the left to not be seen by Robert. Across the hall from the office and locked room, was a small linen closet that they could hide in without being detected. It was a tight fit, but they were able to peak between the wooden blinds on the door.

Just as they inched the door shut behind them, a figure came out of the office and walked to the locked door.

"Is that hi–" Ashley's question was cut off by Melody's hand, and in good time as the figure looked around.

After a slight pause, the figure pulled a key from their pocket and placed it in the lock. They pressed on it and opened the door.

Melody and Ashley were only able to see a slight look at the inside of the room. Nothing out of the normal–an armoire, a rocking chair, and a bed. It was what Melody could see on the bed that got her attention and she quickly snapped a photo before the figure could be heard slamming things in the room and growling in frustration. They ran back out of the room and locked the door once more, before going into the office and disheveling papers in a hurry as if looking for something.

The girls didn't want to wait to find out. They quietly opened the door to the linen closet and jogged up the stairs to avoid detection. Footsteps were heard not far behind them, as they gently held the doorknob to their room and pushed the door shut.

They ran to their beds and pulled their blankets over their heads. The footsteps were near their door, and they each held their breath as the figure cracked it open to check in on them. Not seeing any movement they shut the door once more, and the girls were finally able to exhale.

Melody's and Ashley's hearts were racing, and neither wanted to comment on what they had just witnessed nor about the fear that was smashing into them. They lay awake to listen to the pacing of the footsteps below and the chains that sounded like it was right there with them.

Chapter Sixteen

June 30

I need to write this here so that I can remember to find out more.

Last night as we saw a dark figure in Robert's office, I was able to get a quick picture of what was in the room. It's barely noticeable in the picture, but for that split second in the photo, I was able to see chains on the wall of the room.

They were placed near a dingy mattress, and there were piles of plates underneath.

Is someone living there? Or worse, did Robert kidnap Mara and lock her up in the spare room?

Break in the Case:

- Chains in the locked room
- Food supply
- Mysterious sounds coming from servants' passageway—how to get in?

MM

July

Chapter Seventeen

"Rise and shine, Darlings!" Patrice's voice rang up the stairwell, "That's what everyone's saying, I think, right?"

Melody and Ashley sat up and looked at each other with weary stares.

"Do you remember falling asleep last night?" Ashley glanced toward the doorway.

"Right, girls?" Patrice started walking off into the distance muttering to herself. "I can't ever keep up with all the young lingo anymore...".

Ashley got up and walked over to Melody's bed. "Was it all just a dream? Did someone really come into our room last night?"

Melody kept staring at the beige wall behind Ashley's bed.

"Mel?" Ashley shook Melody back to reality, "Mel!"

"What? Huh? Oh, yea, yea, someone definitely followed us back up here."

"Was it your step dad or your mom, do you think?" Ashley grew concerned over just how far Robert would take to keep that area off limits.

Melody was back to staring at the wall, oblivious to anything Ashley was saying.

"Melody Meltront, why do you keep ignoring me!"

"Oh, sorry, Ash," Melody glanced from Ashley back to the wall, "I was just imagining putting my head in a blender at the idea of my mom referencing the Kardashians even one more time."

Melody's eyes rolled from one side to the other and with that Melody got up out of bed and proceeded to put her clothing on at the dresser. She slipped her legs into her jeans and black dress shirt.

"If I had to guess, I'd say it was Robert. Patrice would never be up that late after drinking her evening wine. She passes out like no one else I've ever seen."

Ashley nodded her head in agreement, "You're mom does have a slight problem."

"Yea, if alcoholism was only a *slight* problem," she snarled, "I hope to never end up like that mess of a woman."

Melody motioned for Ashley to follow her down to breakfast. Ashley quickly put a headband on and ran after Melody. The girls walked into the room. The atmosphere felt different—lighter and relaxed instead of draining. They sat in their seats and looked over at Robert's spot.

"Where is he?" Ashley mouthed across the table.

Melody shrugged and moved her eyes next to Patrice, "Where's Robert on this oh so fine day, mother?"

"Melody, I beg of you please don't antagonize Robert or me today. I just can't handle the stress you are sending through every single one of my nerves this summer," Patrice gently placed the back of her hand to her forehead and slowly wiped it down as if she was removing all the frustration. "You're the one who told me that you would behave as long as you brought your little friend along, um-Ainsley ain't it, darling?

Ashley quit tearing through her eggs that Merna had placed in front of her during the conversation, and looked up to correct Patrice; her finger in the air and mouth agape.

"Mom, first off, her name is Ashley," Melody said for Ashley. "You've known her for nine years."

"That's what I said darling!" The prestigious New York elite accent pushed hard on the 'ah' in 'darling'. She picked up her large chardonnay and gulped it down.

"I just can't with you," Melody rocked her neck from side to side to slowly ease the anger seething inside of her. "Anyway, second of all, I'm simply just asking where he is. He brings down the tone of the room, and I'm glad that it's a little more chipper in here, is all".

Patrice forcefully placed the glass down onto the table–every drop drained down her throat. "Melody, I have had it with you. I'm going to go up to the sunroom and plan more for the party. You two do whatever pleases you, but stay out of our hair until this party is over. I don't want to be getting any more gray hairs than you have already graced me with," she slid her large ornately carved chair back and stood up to brush off her Versace houndstooth dress. "Bernie, another glass of chardonnay! Bring the bottle to the sunroom, immediately!" She belted out before exiting the room.

"Right away, Mrs. Drewmore," the butler hastened his pace to the kitchen to fetch another bottle.

"Two bottles down, three to go," Melody stated mockingly.

"Hey, Mel, quick ask Bernie about the passageway entrances in the chambers!"

Bernie came bustling out of the kitchen and back into the dining room.

"Bernie, we have a question to ask you," Melody shouted at him as he walked through the next door to the main entranceway.

"Ah, young ladies of the manor, I'll find you when I'm done. The monster awaits her liquid diet!" He joked before he rounded the corner and ran up the stairs.

Ashley and Melody looked at each other and busted out laughing at him roasting Patrice. "Yup, that sums it up here," Ashley giggled.

Three hours later Bernie came to find them as they had meandered outside to the garden, and sat near the large stone fountain where a lion spurted water from its mouth.

"There you ladies are! I've been scouring every corner to find you two." He appeared to be out of breath, as his outfit was ruffled and his face reddened from the walk. His black suit made him burn in the summer sun.

"Take a seat Bernie, you look frazzled," Ashley motioned for him to have her seat as she stood up.

"No, no, miss, I could nev–"

Melody interrupted, "Bernie, sit down, it's not like we're *them*. You deserve it, I won't tell anybody."

"Thank you, Melody, you really are just like your father through and through," he pulled out his kerchief and dabbed his brow. "Anyways, what is this burning question you girls have for me, today?" His brow furrowed with concern.

Ashley spoke first, "We got this book yesterday on the manor, and it shows that there is a servant's quarters, in the walls with an entrance through the chambers," her eyes gleamed, wanting to find out more about the mystery of the home.

"Really, we're just trying to find out what Robert's hiding in the locked room next to his office," Melody chimed in, throwing her hand over her shoulder to point her thumb in the manor's direction.

"Oh, Miss Melody, I really wish you wouldn't do your detective routine around Mr. Drewmore. He doesn't seem like the sort of man who likes to be messed with, you know. It's really best if we just keep to ourselves and let him continue." Bernie looked harder at Melody. A smile formed slightly.

"What is it Bernie?" Melody wondered. The slight breeze

"You know, you have your father's determination, but sometimes things are better left hidden. If he has something in that room, I don't want to be the one to have helped you uncover it, especially if it means something could happen to you," Bernie's eyes skimmed the ground in front of him on his last sentence.

"Nothing's going to happen to me, Berns. But..."

"But what, Mel?" Ashley asked.

"On the other hand, Robert, I'm going to find a way to get him out of this family for good." Melody had a spark of fire light in her brown eyes, one that Ashley and Bernie had seen many times before when anything got in her way.

"Bernie, it's just best to let a girl do what she's going to do. There's no stopping her at this point," Ashley's lips tilted to one side of her face as she puckered her mouth in a disapproving way. "She's too hard-headed."

"I better be the one to show you girls than you finding it out and getting caught faster, I guess," Bernie sighed. "Well, let's start with where they are." Bernie stood up and brushed off his black trousers.

Bernie motioned for them to follow as he explained. "Master Meltront—your father's grandfather—never wanted the help to be seen except when needed. He had the stairwell built in the center of the manor to be a way for us to get to each room without entering the hallways as we passed from the kitchen to the rooms. After a while, he then slowly made our housing quarters inside as well. This period became a depressing time for us, as we began to feel isolated being stuck in the walls for our entire time here."

"That sounds awful! How could they do that?" Ashley inquired. Her forehead scrunch is disbelief, "Don't they have laws against that?"

"The pay was so good none of us could turn it down, even if we wanted. We had mouths to feed at our respective homes, despite never seeing our families in return." Bernie's face grew grim. "Master Meltront ran a tight ship, and as long as he was pleased we were well endowed in financial aspects.

The girls looked at each other and nodded as they understood that money talks.

Bernie continued, "Anyway, I'm getting off topic, each room has a passageway that leads to this old staircase, but when your father inherited it, he made sure to block off the majority of the doors. The ones he allowed to stay open were the ones in the lower chambers and the one in the room next to his. He said in case there was anything precious that needed to be hidden—including your family in chances of a break in."

"Well, that would explain why Robert has it locked. He must be hiding something in the walls," Melody looked again at Bernie, "We keep hearing these sounds in the walls, it's as if they're right on the other side of my room's wall, I have to know what's inside there."

"I'm starting to be quite alright, if we just drop this case," Ashley chirped.

"Noises in the walls?" Bernie's forehead creased from confusion.

"It sounds like a chain being dragged against it," Melody paused, "I think he's traveling through the stairwell at night. He has to be."

"I guess, I can take your girls to explore just this once while he's out for the day. But, promise that you will never tell a living soul, because it'll be off with my head and job if Mr. Drewmore finds out," Bernie's face grew serious, a side that Melody only saw at times of trouble in the family.

"I promise, Bernie, I just want to make sure it's worth it to continue the investigation on him."

"All right, right this way." Bernie led them back inside the manor, and straight to a door that was placed between the two staircases of the main balcony before them. It was hidden by large potted palms that blocked the door, and featured a lion's head etched into the wall. If one didn't know any better they would assume it to be only a carving. Bernie's eyes darted around to make sure nobody saw them, and he twisted the lion's head to the right and the doorway pushed in and slid inward.

Ashley's mouth fell open, and Melody's eyes looked shocked as she had never seen such a thing in all her years.

Bernie brought them inside and quickly closed the doorway. In front of them was a second set of steps that paved the way to an open area where a tan colored stone lined the walls and floors To the right a large portrait of Master Meltront was hung. Bernie unhooked the large gold frame and placed it gingerly on the floor. Behind it was a wooden door that was simply carved and had years of cobwebs overlaying it.

"Here's the answer to your question, ladies. I have to hurry back up before your mother needs a refill. I already went out after breakfast to gather more party supplies, but I'll be going again soon for more wine," Bernie waved them off .

"Thanks, Bernie!" The girls shouted after him as he ran up the steps."

"Be careful, ladies, and don't get caught!" Bernie warned.

Melody opened the wooden door and years worth of dust escaped out and into the girls' eyes. Ashley gasped for breath, as the dirt landed in her throat. "Oh, my lanta," she coughed into her hands, "I don't think this stairwell is good for our health," she managed to say before going into another coughing fit.

Together the girls walked into the doorway and up the stairs. They checked the three small eight by ten living quarters in the basement. Each only contained a small, dingy cot, and a tiny dresser with a lamp on it. Hardly a place for a person to live. The walls felt cold and the air was musty.

Ashley's fingertips graced the moss that edged its way higher and higher up the corridor. It felt damp and bristly. *Just like in a fairytale home.*

They neared their way to the door that led to the locked room, when all of a sudden they heard the door slam upstairs.

The girls ran back out of the stairwell, making sure to put the picture back into place, and ran up the steps. Through a small peephole in the lion's mouth they were able to watch as Robert glanced around the room and walked upstairs to his room.

Melody let out a sigh of relief, as she waited a few minutes and then opened up the wall to come out.

"Come with me for a summer, " she said. It'll be fun, she said. Oh, you know, just a boring area and nothing to worry about, she said," Ashley ran down the list as her eyes grew wild. "I'm beginning to think it was all a ploy, and you knew from the start this wasn't going to be a relaxing summer in the swamps," Ashley crossed her arms over her chest and huffed.

"What can I say, mystery just follows me," Melody smirked, as if all the red flags going off in her brain meant for her to continue on her manhunt. "Let's just wait a little longer and wait until we hear that sound again. It shouldn't be but a couple more days. In the meantime, we have a party to plan!"

The way that Melody said it rubbed Ashley the wrong way and she knew that something was brewing.

Melody smiled at her friend, and thought to herself: *And a little planning to get Robert to expose himself, while we're at it, to icing the cake.*

Chapter Eighteen

July 2nd

Dear Diary,

Today, Bernie showed us the hidden passageway for the old servant's quarters. How awful is it to think the staff were forced to live in the walls? It was neat seeing the walls come to life, though, as the door slid open and exposed a large room that led to another hidden section.

This place has so many secrets and I'm positive if the walls could talk, they'd be screaming out what Robert's hiding. He wasn't at breakfast this morning, which is not his typical character. Patrice is all out of sorts, and is running around looking for decorations like a chicken with her head chopped off.

I've never been to a party that requires so much planning and decor...I'm excited to see what it's all about though, as I wanted to see what the hubbub is about. I think they call it hobnobbing in their world? Idk, but it's something different, and I'm willing to try most things once....or twice, if Melody's in charge.

In other world news, I was called Ainsley today. I haven't heard that one before. Melody's mother has known me for all these years and still can't remember my name. Sometimes I wonder if the alcohol has seeped completely through her brain. Other times, I wonder if she does it out of spite, or simply because she doesn't care about me enough to remember my name.

Either way, it's time for bed. I have a long weekend ahead of me as I view the world of the rich through the eye's of the poor.

As Always,
Ashley

Chapter Nineteen

Bright and early, Melody had been the last one to bed, and the first one to rise. She had her notebook out with doodles drawn through it about ways to get Robert to oust himself.

Approaches

1. *Pull out the vial and book on Mara right in front of everybody at the dinner table.*

2. *Have a slideshow start on the tv screen during cocktails*

3. *Bring up Mara to their friends; ask questions*

4. *Make up the worst case scenario, and see if he backtracks on details*

5. *WWDD?*

Ashley leaned over Melody's shoulder, "WWDD? What does that stand for?"

"What Would Dexter Do, of course. Could it possibly mean anything else?"

Ashley smacked her forehead with her palm, "I should have listened to all those people who used to tell me you're strange," she said with a smile.

"Ahh yes, the ones who are afraid to be different. They're just upset they can't be as cool as me."

"Mel, I think the correct terminology would be insane," Ashley tried saying it with a straight face, but couldn't hold her laughter towards her own joke.

"Ha-Ha, very funny. Anyway get back to helping me, goon! I need to figure out what the best plan of action would be to take Robert down." Melody slammed her right hand into her left fist.

"Well, first off, let's just scratch out that whole worst case scenario scene. I don't think he'd be willing to divulge any information. Bu-uuut, I do think he would be willing to throw you under the bus, and say you're a liar."

Melody nodded in agreement and crossed it out.

"Also, I don't think we truly have enough information to just willy nilly pull out the vial and book. I mean, what are you going to say: *I found this medicine that can cause a person to slowly die, which means he killed my father?*" Ashley asked Melody.

"I guess you're right on that one too. We have the book though! He can't deny facts. Why would he be hiding all of those clippings, and then it had details of their affair," Melody paused to think of more evidence.

"They're not going to ostracize him for an affair, Mel...," Ash's voice trailed off as Melody remembered something important.

"It wasn't just articles, though, Ash. I looked through all of the pages later that night," Melody said as her face turned somber.

A lump formed in Melody's throat as she struggled to get the words out of her mouth.

"There's no good way for me to say it, so I'll just say it. Ash, there was hair with blood on it in there between two pages. It had a fingerprint in blood."

Ashley's eyes widened, "Mel, this isn't just fun and games anymore! We have to tell somebody!"

Ashley paced the wood boards and her body trembled.

"This. This...," Ashley paused to gather her thoughts and her hand slowly wandered to her mouth as she chewed at her nails.

"Blah, blah, blah. That's all I keep hearing. But I want to make him admit his crimes and ruin his career. I want to cut him where it hurts most, and that's working at the university." Melody circled her plan to show the evidence at the party,

Ashley stopped in the middle of the room, "This is serious, Mel!"

"I know this is serious! I'm going to make him regret inserting himself into the father role, and I'll ensure that there's a video of the whole thing so when he admits to it he can't backtrack." She closed the little black notebook, and jumped out of her bed.

"I don't know, it seems pretty dangerous," Ashley continued to pick at her cuticles. She didn't want to fully accept that Melody gave her a role in this scheme.

"It's dangerous for *him*. Dexter always played the long game when needed, and sometimes you just have to put the lobster in boiling water to see how long it takes them to jump out.

"What if you're the lobster?" Ashley pointed out.

"I'm the chef," Melody said pointedly. "Now, let's invite our new friend to the show. How about a ride to town?" Melody turned towards the open doorway and shouted through the halls, "Bernie! Start the car!"

Chapter Twenty

Bernie rushed to the car, and opened the door for the girls. "Where to Miss Melody and Miss Ashley?"

"Oh, Berns, stop calling me 'Miss'," moaned Melody.

"Sorry Mi-, I mean Melody. Where would you two like to go today?" Bernie asked.

"We want to go to the bookstore in town," Ashley chimed in.

"Ah, yes, Mrs. Annie's bookstore. What a lovely woman. You know your father and she used to be friends," Bernie lifted his eyes to the rearview mirror, "That was until Mrs. Drewmore put an end to it."

Melody stared Ashley dead in the eyes, "Motive number one," she whispered before she turned back towards Bernie's stare. "I know she had mentioned Dad helped her with opening her store, but I didn't know it was anything more than that."

"Do you remember the vow to secrecy you always made me do when you were little?" Bernie kept his eyes on the road.

"Yes, Bern, why?"

"There's something you should know, and I'm afraid that if Mrs. Drewmore were to find out, I'd be in a disappearing act. I need a vow that you two will never tell another soul about this," Bernie looked back up and gave a look of trust knowing that Melody would never divulge the details.

"Promise," the girls replied in unison.

Over the next five minutes, the girls heard the story of how Dan and Annie had met in high school.

"They were high school sweethearts. Even won the best couple status for senior year," Bernie recalled. "It was once Mr. Meltront moved to Yale that everything fell apart for them."

"Why was that?" Ashley asked, entertained by the story.

"Well, Mr. Meltront, he had been accepted to Yale on a scholarship—he hadn't quite gotten the manor and the wealth with it at that point. He ended up quickly making friends with his new roommate...Mr. Drewmore."

"That snake! I knew he had something to do with it," Melody sneered.

Bernie nodded. The cypresses passed them on their journey and loomed over the vehicle casting their presence and tone on the situation at hand.

"Well, once they became the best of friends. Mr. Drewmore introduced Mr. Meltront to college life and soon forgot all about Annie who was waiting at home for him. She tried calling and calling, but communications simply ceased."

"I could never see your dad being the type to ghost someone," Ashley commented.

"Me either," Melody agreed.

Bernie continued the story of how Dan ended up falling in love with Patrice at Yale and stayed away for the duration of five years as he built his stockbroker portfolio in New York—far away from the small town of Clinch, Georgia.

The girls sat in silence, not knowing what to say. The town emerged in the distance, and the fog from the swamps dissipated before them. Melody felt sorry for those that lived next to the swamps. It seemed as if the air was always filled with fog and she imagined it to be hard to stay in a place so sticky and hard on the eyes.

Bernie stopped the car in a parking spot near the bookstore, and the girls caught a glimpse of Reed entering the store with his gray beanie snug on his head.

How is he not hot in that thing? Ashley thought.

Bernie leaned against the headrest to continue the story. In the meantime, Master Meltront had died, and the manor had been passed down to his only son–albeit estranged he was the next of kin—only to have it then released to Dan since his father had no interest in ever going back to that 'monstrosity'. Dan decided that he needed a break from the big life of the city, and chose to spend the summer with his family at his new manor.

"It was nice catching up at first, for your father, and by the second summer he spent here he had rekindled a friendship with Annie. Summer turned to fall, fall to winter, and so on, until Mr. Meltront decided that maybe stockbroking wasn't for him, anymore," Bernie rattled on.

"Dad never was about money over family," Melody recounted.

Bernie paused with a small smile, "Anyway. When your dad decided to move here permanently, it meant that Patrice was here, too. And, well...she didn't like that. You're dad would secretly say he had to meet with business partners who had come down to get him to sign papers every now and then, but in reality, he was with Annie," he stopped again, and glanced back at the girls, "I'm sorry Miss Melody, I hope I'm not saying too much, but I–I just...," Bernie stuttered.

"What happened, Bernie? Did Patrice find out?" Melody questioned calmly.

"You see. Mrs. Drewmore didn't like that your father and Annie were becoming all chummy again, and she hired an investigator to get pictures for proof. And that he did. Your father didn't want to embarrass Mrs. Drewmore, but he was in love with Mrs. Annie."

Ashley's mouth was slowly falling open as all of the details swirled. "Melody, I'm starting to think your father really was murdered."

"Continue Bernie, what happened next?" Melody was no longer herself, and in her mind her detective deduction crept out.

"I believe you were about eight years old, Miss Melody," Bernie recalled. His brows furrowed at the memory.

Bernie then told them how Patrice found out about the affair.

"What is this?" Patrice shoved papers into Dan's chest.

Dan unfolded the crumpled forms and straightened them out. He scrunched his face and dared not to look at Patrice. "They look like divorce papers."

"Divorce papers?" Patrice shrieked as she stomped in her red Jimmy Choos. "Divorce papers! As if you're anything without me! How dare you embarrass me like this."

"Patrice, will you please calm down, and talk about this rationally?" Dan pleaded, his eyebrows knitted and his voice slow and even. "You know we're not happy living like this. Why stay in something when you're not happy?"

"Happy? Who needs happiness? At this point our relationship is a staple for showing stable marriages to our fans," Patrice scoffed.

"Fans? I don't live my life for clicks on social media, Patrice," Dan's hands hovered while he tried to get Patrice to have reason, "I found someone...."

His eyes focused back on the floors of the foyer to the manor.

"Oh, darling, there's never going to be someone other than me," she said as she folded her arms.

"Patrice, I have nothing left in me to fight with. Just sign the divorce papers, and let's move on for our sake and Melody's," he begged.

"You're leaving me for *her* aren't you," her voice showed she knew exactly who he was with.

"Yes...," Dan confirmed in a whisper.

"If I can't have you, she won't either!" Patrice threw the papers back at Dan.

They fell to his feet, and Dan knelt down to pick them up.

Bernie snuck his head in from the dining room door.

"Master Meltront, is the coast clear?" Bernie asked.

"It's Dan. And yes, she's gone," Dan said lightly.

"If my opinion were to ever matter, I do think you've made the right choice Master... erm, Dan." Bernie picked up the remaining papers, shifted them into a neat stack, and handed them back to Dan.

Dan nodded his head. He knew that this was inevitable, and Patrice was going to have to learn a life without him.

Bernie looked at the girls, "Before your father could get your mother to sign the papers, he grew ill, and while Mrs. Annie did try to come see him, Mrs. Drewmore made sure that the guards in the hospital kicked her out." Bernie stopped and looked down at the floor, "He died and your mom got everything."

Melody took a moment to gather her thoughts. She didn't know what to say or how to feel. Her body tingled because the mystery now had more pieces, but numb because she knew the awful truth about their marriage. *Did the vial play a part in Dad's murder? Who is to blame Patrice...Robert...both?*

"I think I need a minute," she proceeded to calmly get out of the car, and as she gently closed the door behind her, Melody cried hard for the first time in a while.

Melody cried because she missed her father. She cried because she hated being near Patrice and Robert. She cried because her mother was hungry for money and fame, when all her father wanted was for something real. The tears dripped down her face, as the rain fell covering up their trail.

Ashley got out of the car, and ran to her friend, as she pulled her into a tight embrace and allowed Melody to sob into her shoulder. Ashley gave Bernie a look of sadness, and Bernie felt as if he had said too much.

Melody got her emotions back into their box and walked over to Bernie who was now standing in front of the vehicle. She hugged him, and quietly whispered the words, "thank you". Bernie nodded, not wanting to push buttons, and watched as the girls walked into the bookstore.

Reed noticed the girls before they spotted him as he hid behind the racks of books. He peeked through the slots staring Ashley in the eye, "Boo!" he shouted and then popped his head above the shelves.

Ashley jumped in fear, "Oh my goodness! Don't you ever do that again, I almost had a heart attack!" Her hand placed over her heart as the beat palpated through the chest's wall.

"Quit being a baby, we have bigger fish to fry," she said as she locked eyes with Reed. "Where's your mom?"

"She ran next door to the diner to grab lunch for us, I bet if we leave now we can catch her, and you guys could joi-" Reed was cut off by Melody's glare. "Well you look like you're having a Wednesday Addams kinda day, huh, Miss Depressing Pants."

His attempt at a joke was wasted on Melody who wanted no parts of it.

Melody took a step in his direction and pointed her finger right at him, "Do you know anything about your mom and my dad?"

"Uhm, I mean well yeah mom tells me everything," he gulped, "Could you, uh, could you please get your finger out of my face?"

"Mel, come on! Back it up tiger, he has nothing to do with this!" Ashley attempted to wrangle Melody without success.

"What do you know?" She lowered her finger, but her stare intensified, showing all the darker flecks of brown in her still glistening eyes. "Tell me now!"

"I think it's best if we just wait for my mom...," Reed felt hot, and his palms began to sweat as he looked for a way out.

DING!

The door to the bookstore opened and through it came Mrs. Annie. "Ah, nice to see you again girls," she exclaimed before looking over at her son, and her smile faded, "What is happening here?"

"Mom, I think you need to tell Melody about you know what."

Annie sighed and placed her purse on the counter before turning back in their direction. "What do you want to know?"

For an hour, Annie discussed the events that led to her and Dan rekindling their relationship. While it wasn't something that Melody willingly wanted to learn, she had to for the sake of finding out the truth of what happened. Her emotions welled up inside her like tidal waves.

Melody was too prideful to cry in front of people, except those who she was closest to, and this time would be no different. That is until the moment her limit of keeping everything locked up inside was reached and her body finally fought back as she ran outside to vomit right as Annie finished the topic of the affair.

Melody gathered herself once more and walked back into the store, and said the first words, "Do you think my dad would still be here if it weren't for Patrice?" Her eyes twinkled with tears.

"I don't want to place the blame on Patrice, but I do think that a lot of the stress that he faced before his illness caused it. I think without the stress, he wouldn't have gotten so sick, so fast," Annie paused and looked at Melody and admired how strong and bold she was. "You know you remind me of him, in a way. The way you stand up for a cause no matter the pain. He did that too." Her eyes went to the floor on the last sentence.

"I hear that a lot," Melody's smile slowly appeared and then quickly faded as soon as it had come. "Did you ever know my mother on a personal level? Or hear about her?"

"We weren't friends, but I did hear stories about her. Stories about her family and their desire to gain more wealth. Your dad told me that she placed more importance on money than family, and that's one of the things that drew them apart. Nobody really *liked* Patrice, but more so tolerated her so as to not upset her."

"Do you think she could kill someone, though?" Ashley questioned.

"Oh, never!" Annie exclaimed. "I don't think she's dangerous or willing to do anything that would tarnish her family's name," she said as she defended Patrice—something Melody could never force herself to do. "What I could see, if your father was still alive, is her exacting revenge. She has a jealous spirit, and I think that if your father and I had been together now, she would have wanted to make both of us miserable. Kind of like if she can't have him, I couldn't be happy."

Melody finally looked for Ashley, only to realize that Reed and her had snuck off outside to be in a more joyful setting. She looked out the door at them as Ashley laughed at something Reed said, and Reed gently placed his hand on her shoulder smiling. *At least one of us is happy*.

"Melody, can I ask you something?"

Melody nodded.

"Why is it that you care so much about something that never came to fruition? It's not like I was with your father in his final days–although I had tried so hard. Why are you digging in the past?"

Melody looked at Annie's eyes for the first time as she noticed all the wrinkles that lined the corners of her eyes. She thought about all of the memories that could have been made, and how one event caused catastrophe. Melody thought about the possibility of growing up with Annie as a mother figure and how she would be away from the grips of her mother.

She stood there in silence as she pondered all that could have been, and glanced back up to Annie, "Because the past found me,"

Annie pulled Melody in for a hug, and they swayed for a minute as Melody inhaled the aroma of Annie's perfume.

How I wish I had the opportunity to know you, Melody thought as she pulled away. "I think I better get back home, I don't want to keep Bernie gone too long. He might get in trouble. Would it be okay if Reed came with us for dinner?"

Annie closed her eyes for a second to think about any harm it could do, and with a peaceful inhale and exhale she spoke, "That'll be all right, but make sure he calls me to check in!".

"Thank you," Melody said as walked outside to her friends. "Hey, Reed, your mom said it was okay if you came with us for dinner. She said to just make sure you check in with her."

Reed looked back at his mom, smiled and waved, and then the three set off to the car to begin the ride home.

Chapter Twenty One

The swamp lands cast a thick fog on the way to the manor, and as the car pulled into the long driveway, the gloomy trees emitted an eerie image on the outside. The gray stone walls seemed like they were crying from the mist, with two enormous weeping willows splayed on each side.

Ashley began to get a strange feeling that something was amiss and her body shuddered at the thought of staying there anymore.

A glow from the front step's light bulb shined down the stairwell, as the girls and Reed clamored out of the back of the Royce, and up to the door.

"Man, your house has the same vibe as you, Melody," Reed chuckled.

"Ha. Ha," Melody rolled her eyes and pushed open the large doors, "Like I haven't heard that one before."

"I said the same thing...," Ashley leaned in and whispered to Reed.

"One could get lost in here," Reed expressed before being cut off by Robert as he entered the foyer.

"Ahh, yes, one could most definitely get *lost* in here," he placed a hand on Reed's shoulder. The bony structure of Robert's hands accentuated his long fingers, and Reed turned to look at it, feeling every desire inside of him telling him to leave. "Make sure you don't venture near the office. I'm sure Melody will tell you all about it," Robert's voice was dripping with charm, as he attempted to show his good side to the new guest.

He removed his hand from Reed's shoulder and placed it in front of him to offer a handshake.

"Yes, sir. I'm Reed by the way," the trembling in his voice gave away his weakness.

"Hi, Reed. I"m Mr. Drewmore, but you can call me Robert. It's nice to see a young fellow around the house, Melody never brings anybody home except Miss Ashley here." He glanced at Ashley and then back to Reed. "So Mr. Reed, what sorts of things are you interested in? Sports? Books? Theater?" His perfectly kept eyebrows raised hoping for the correct answer.

"Uh, books, sir. My mom actually owns-"

"His mom owns a huge collection of vintage books," Melody interjected.

Reed looked at Ashley, then they all stared at Melody.

"Oh, really? Well that's fantastic! A man of culture, I say. It's always nice to hear that young people are still into books. You're a dying breed young man."

Reed nodded in agreement, unsure of what to say.

"What's your favorite book, Reed?" Robert asked as he placed his hands into the pockets of his gray trousers. It matched well with his forest green sweater.

"*Hamlet*," while Reed could only muster out one word, it was the right word to chip away at Robert.

"I would not say I'm a fan of Shakespeare, but I do remember the play well from my university days," Robert paused, and gathered his words, "A strange interest for a young man of what sixteen? Eighteen?"

"Eighteen, sir," the lump in Reed's throat was finally pushed down to his stomach.

"Hmm, I might have to keep an eye on you.." Robert's voice faded off.

"Robert!" Patrice called from the sitting room. "Robert!" she shouted once more with anger.

"Any who, I better go. Just know I'm always watching you three," he began to walk away and turned back one final time to give them a quick lookover, and exited the room.

Reed was able to breathe a sigh of relief. "Jesus, you two didn't tell me you had Lurch for a stepfather. That man gives me goosebumps." He rubbed his folded arms.

"Get used to it, Melody loves to put her friends in awkward situations," Ashley scoffed.

"Come one you two, we need to go where nobody will hear."

The three walked up the staircase and down the hall to Melody's room.

Reed passed by the pictures on the walls. One featured a large man in a Revolutionary era suit. It reminded Reed of pictures of Napoleon in his attire, but less little-man syndrome. The eyes on the painting seemed to travel with the gang as they passed by, and Reed could sense that coming here wasn't the best idea.

Ashley and Reed went into the room and Melody closed the door behind her. "All right, here's the deal, Reed. We're in a little predicament. We are restricted from going into his office. Keyword: "we"," she placed both her pointer fingers and thumbs together into a gun shape as she talked, "And well, I need something out of there to get a confession."

"And where exactly do I come into play?"

"We're going to distract and keep an eye out while you look for the evidence, of course," Melody looked at Reed with a slight smirk.

"We?" Ashley stammered.

"Precisely, my dear." The look on Melody's face told her friends that she was in it until the mystery was solved.

"Nah, I'm good, I think I'm just going to go home."

Just as he said that Bernie knocked on the door, and cracked it ever so slightly.

"Miss Melody, I came to let your friend know that the fog has set in and unfortunately it might be late into the night before it ascends. I think it would be best to call his mom and let her know that I will bring him home first thing in the morn," Bernie tipped his black hat and closed the door.

"Just my darn luck," Reed said.

Reed paced the floorboards, as he called his mother and told her the news. She reluctantly agreed after a ten-minute discussion and said that he must be home first thing. Annie didn't like him being so close to the family, and Reed was beginning to see why.

"I guess, I'll do it. But if I get caught, I'm never coming back here again, and I'm telling them it's all your fault," he exclaimed.

"That's what I used to say," Ashley quietly chimed in as she picked the skin around her fingernails.

Melody went over the plan again and again until everybody could recite it. They would wait until bedtime, and sneak down to the office. Reed would take a flashlight and look for a book that was labeled "MARA".

"Do not, and I can't express this enough, DO NOT open the book!" Melody warned.

"All right, all right, I got it. Don't open the book," He placed his head into his hands, and rubbed his forehead from the stress.

She continued on as she discussed that Ashley would be pretending to get a glass of water. This meant that Melody would be standing at the end of the hallway. If she was to see Robert approach, she would whistle. The whistle would be Reed's alert to exit the office and enter the linen closet across the hallway, and let Ashley know to begin to walk down the hallway as if she had just got the water.

"Hopefully, you're quick," Melody squinted her eyes at Reed, "I know how boys like to be slow on the details."

"And just where do you expect me to start in the office to look for this book?" Reed figured if he presented immediate fails to the plan he wouldn't have to execute it, but boy was he wrong.

"Once you walk in, go to the left side of the study, and it'll be on the bottom row. I forget quite where I placed it the last time I was able to get in there."

"Why can't you just wait until the next opportunity for you to sneak in there?" Reed asked.

"The party's tomorrow, and I'm going to show Robert just who he's dealing with," Melody insisted.

Ashley looked at Melody as the mystery was beginning to force its hooks all the way into her. Ashley felt that there was no good ending planned for this case, but she was forced to stick it out as there was no way to go back home. She was always loyal to a fault, and couldn't imagine bailing on Melody in her time of closure, but she couldn't help that the tingling in her body wouldn't stop and that her heart raced like a horse on an endless track.

Ashley looked over at Reed, and placed her hand next to his. Their fingertips barely touched, but butterflies exploded in her stomach at the feeling. *At least he's here with me, I don't have to face all the intimidating parts alone*, she thought.

Reed continued to look at Melody, but calmly placed his hand on Ashley's; she melted at the touch, and she was ready to take on the next adventure.

The lights faded around the manor as each person went to bed. Reed was given a room on the bottom east wing, so he could not easily access the girls' room. Melody and Ashley pretended to turn in.

The manor was dark, and all that could be heard were the sounds of the home settling.

Reed lay in the bed, and while the room was inviting with the lights on, it had the opposite effect when in complete darkness. His room had no ambient light casted on the walls like the girls, and outside the hooting of an owl made him think about every horror story he had ever read. *This is not how horror stories start. This is not how they start.*

Upstairs, the girls were quietly getting out of bed. Ashley reached to the nightstand and texted Reed they were ready. They tiptoed down the staircase and peered into the east wing waiting for the shadowy figure at the end of the hall to quicken his pace.

Reed got to the girls and Melody instantly thrust a flashlight into his hands. "Here, you take this and hurry it up."

"Use your nice words," Reed sarcastically exclaimed.

"Ugh, please, hurry up!" She pushed him in the direction of the office, and looked over to Ashley, "All right now you go right down there, and when you hear my whistle start walking with the glass as if you were coming from the kitchen."

Melody stood in the center of the wings and the eerie glow from the skylight shone down. *This place might be a little creepy like Ashley says…*

Melody glanced over at the office and could barely make out the dim light as Reed searched the row of books. She tapped her foot in impatience, just as a door from upstairs faintly closed.

Phwwwwhht!

The whistle was soft, but managed to alert the others. Robert casually walked down the staircase, eyes locked on Melody. Her eyes steadily followed him, but did a quick side glance to see Reed as he showed her the book in his hands, and he popped into the closet.

Behind her the footsteps of Ashley approached, as Robert stood directly in front.

"And just what are you doing here? Trying to sneak into my office? Tsk, tsk." His slicked hair contrasted well with the moonlight shimmering in. "I thought you knew better than that."

"No, I have no desire to enter your office, *Robert*," the words rolled off her tongue in a way that made it want to retract down her throat and burn itself in the acids of her stomach. "Actually, I'm here to help Ashley. She doesn't like the darkness of the manor and prefers to have someone walk with her. I chose to stay here as a meeting point. That is if you really wanted to know," she narrowed her eyes, "Besides, I think I should be asking you what you are doing up at this late hour?"

"Your mother's snoring has rendered me the opportunity to be restless tonight," he looked over at the office door and saw it cracked slightly. "I figured I'd read a little Chaucer to get back to it." Robert locked eyes with Ashley, "Anyway, off to bed you two, we have an important day tomorrow." He extended his arm out and guided them up the stairs.

"That we do," Melody replied. *That we do.*

The girls got to their room, and shut the door behind them. They went to the bay window and Ashley pulled out her phone.

Ashley: Did you make it back to your room?

Reed: Safe and sound

Ashley: Good :)

Ashley: Make sure you hide the book.

Reed: Will do (:

Ashley looked at the smiley face, and her stomach fluttered.

Melody saw the 'look', "Oh, please don't tell me you're...," she fake gagged, "You're in love, aghh."

"I'm not in love, I just.. I don't know, I just really like him, I guess," Ashley folded her legs and pulled a pillow up to her chin, "Is that so bad?"

Melody looked out at the moon. The same moon that she and her father used to love looking at everynight through his telescope. "No, I'm glad you have someone else in your life now."

"He's not going to replace you, if that's what you're thinking," she placed her hand on Melody's.

Melody squeezed back, "I'm not worried about that, goon. I just know that things are going to change for us. We have one year left in high school, and I still don't know what I want to do with my life, or where I want to go."

"I told you, you could come with me!" Ashley looked out the window, "I'd really rather prefer you to come with me, because I couldn't imagine that experience without you." Ashley's voice began to tremble.

"You wouldn't want to find normal friends; start over?"

"Of course not!" Ashley furrowed her brow, "why would you ever think that?"

"No reason, but I'm glad either way," Melody cracked a slight smile.

For a few minutes the girls sat in silence together, just taking in the moment.

"Ash, do you ever grieve? I mean, I know your dad didn't die on you, but he abandoned you which is similar in a way, I guess…""Yea, I grieve. I grieve for who my father could've been, and the father he should've been for me. Why do you ask, Mel?"

"Being back here has been hard for me. I can't stop thinking about Dad every second. Everywhere I look, there's a memory that can't be erased and it plays on the walls like the slideshow in my head. For those moments, I can hear his heartbeat, his voice. I begin to imagine what it'd be like to have him here instead of Robert. And I can't stop the intrusive thoughts of what it would be like to have Annie instead of Patrice," Melody held her head, "It's like the thoughts just don't stop, even when I scream at them too."

Melody sobbed into the palms of her hands; her elbows balancing on folded knees.

"I hate to say it, but they never will, Mel. He'll always be with you, and you'll want to remember the good times, but make sure you don't miss the present being in the past. Your dad would never want that for you."

Melody swiped at her tears, "I know," she whispered.

She sat there crying a little longer, until it felt she had run dry, and Ashley walked her to her bed, and held her until she fell asleep.

Chapter Twenty Two

July 3rd

Dear Whoever is Reading this Bullshit,

I'm not really sure what to say here, but I've read Ashley's dumb diary enough to know you always start with dear-something.

Anyway, today's been rough, and Ash said that maybe doing something like this would help ease my emotions. She's normally right on these types of things, and I figured why not.

Today I was told about my father's affair with Reed's mother, Annie. It's something I never saw coming, and while it is a hard subject, I'm glad I know. I never saw my father being the one to cheat on Patrice. Quite frankly, I figured it would have been the other way around, but surprise! Life throws curveballs like Merna said.

I feel that I should be mad, frustrated, or upset for this—and I'm upset, but for all the wrong reasons. I'm upset because my father died unhappy. He died in the arms of Patrice who is so cold-hearted to have made my father stay in a loveless marriage, but also for how much of a hypocrite she is. My father couldn't be happy, yet here's Robert.

If my dad were still alive, I believe that he would be living a happy life here with Annie. She's a little too pleasant of a person—I guess there's someone like Ashley in everyone's life—but she feels like *home*.

I can't describe it either. I've only met her twice, and still I feel like I"ve known her for years.

Here's to all the things we can't change, I guess.

Sincerely or Whatever,

MM

Chapter Twenty Three

The morning of the party came, and the girls rushed downstairs first thing to wake up Reed. To their surprise, Reed was nowhere to be found, and when they went to the dining room, they saw Bernie as he poured orange juice.

"Bernie, where did Reed go?" Ashley asked.

"Master Reed went back home about two hours ago, young ladies. His mother runs a tight ship, and that was the arrangement."

"Oh, yea that's right," Melody mumbled. She elbowed Ashley, "Text him, you know what," she whispered before they dispersed to walk to their respective side of the table.

The atmosphere felt different, and the girls glanced in each direction, before settling on each other.

"Where are they?" Ashley mouthed across the table.

Melody shrugged.

Reed sent back the text they all wanted to know.

Reed: Look behind the radiator

Merna entered the room to serve breakfast, just as the girls stood up to leave. "Sorry, Merna!" Ashley quipped.

Melody ran past Merna and through the doors to the front of the manor, "We're on a case!"

Ashley looked to Merna with a sympathetic glance before exiting, and Merna shook her head from side-to-side as she already knew, "That girl and her cases. I swear she's never going to find a lad around here to keep up."

By the time that Ashley reached the guest room, Melody was already standing at the radiator motioning for her to close the door. Ashley looked down the hallway and saw nobody coming, she stepped back into the room and quietly closed the door behind her.

Melody picked up the book from between the radiator and wall, and looked at it in her hands. "Here's the evidence to get him out of our hair for good!"

"Now, just how do you plan to get that out of this room and into ours until tonight?" Ashley questioned.

Melody looked around the room, and located a rainbow macrame purse from when Patrice went through her Bohemian phase. "We'll use that, but you carry it because it'll look suspicious on me."

"Of course it will," Ashley's anxiety flared up as she created scenarios in her head of what would happen if Robert discovered what the purse held inside. *What if he sees us and asks us what's in there? What do I do then? Why am I the scapegoat?*

"Hello! Earth to Ash," Melody waved her hand in Ashley's face, and Ashley was snapped back to reality.

"Oh, huh?"

"I said, let's go you goon!"

The girls walked briskly to the center of the foyer and looked around. The coast was clear as they began to make the dash upstairs.

"Oh, girls!" Patrice called from the front door.

Patrice's nails were freshly manicured with a floral design and she was waving them for the girls to come closer. Melody reluctantly turned around to get the ordeal over with. Ashley struggled to get her legs to work as they were stuck in fright.

"Yes, mother." Melody's voice showed the displeasure that she faced even being around her.

"I just want to make sure that you girls know to be–" Patrice paused and looked at Ashley, "Do your legs not work anymore girl? Get down here for the conversation," she snapped.

Ashley trudged down the steps, and her legs felt like sandbags as they got heavier with each step. "Sorry, mam."

"Okay, that's better," Patrced said as she pulled up her Chanel sunglasses to the top of her head. "I want to make sure that you girls know to be on your best behavior. Tonight's a night where all our friends will see how hard we work for all of this."

"Yea, work," Melody snorted.

"Excuse me young lady, but Robert and I do work for our money, and I'll have you kn–".

It was at this point that Melody drowned out the words.

Melody peeked out of the corner of her eye to see Ashley shake ever so slightly and knew she had to get her out of there. "We got it, we got it. Be on our best behavior. Be seen, not heard. Yada yada," she spun her fingers in a circular motion, "Now can we please go?"

Patrice hated when Melody talked to her like that, but didn't want to use anymore energy on the situation when she had a party to plan. She turned toward the kitchen and walked away. "Bernie! Bring in my party supplies and start handing them up!" she ordered.

Ashley looked like she saw a ghost, and emotionlessly walked the staircase while she gripped the rails as the whites in her knuckles showed.

The girls got to the room, and Melody locked the door for good measure.

"Here, let's make sure we look at this front to back so we know *everything* we're working with. Robert is a sly one, and he's not getting out of this.

For hours, the two of them delved into each page. Ones contained images of Robert and Merna holding hands. Some were menial and only showed them in the typical professor/TA relationship. When they found the ones that showcased more of the affair than they bargained to see they simply put a placeholder in the page to reference it in case Robert backtracked. Then they got to *the page.*

"This is what creeps me out Mel, why would he keep her hair and why does this look like blood?" Ashley asked as she drew back from the blood touched corners.

"I mean, i don't know," Melody hesitated, "I think if we show these pages though, he won't have an excuse and people will begin to make up their own stories. Patrice won't want him anymore if he's a disgrace to the family name," Melody smirked.

Chapter Twenty Four

The following hour, the girls looked out the upper hall window to see the first cars begin to pull into the driveway. Women wore long sparking cocktail dresses, and they were all escorted by a male in a tux. Melody had grown used to this type of event back in New York, and it didn't phase her to see close to a hundred people guffawing over any new current affair.

"Can you believe the stock market, today? *Dow and Jones* decreased by over 300 points." One man pointed out.

"I heard that we're on the brink of a recession! Can you believe that?" replied a second.

"It's all just a ruse for the Democrats to push out the Republicans in the electoral race, you know. We're not even close to a recession," scoffed the third, "Why, just yesterday I was able to buy a 3.1 million dollar estate on the outskirts of Brooklyn with reasonable interest. That wouldn't be possible if we were on the so-called brink!"

Melody and Ashley were dressed in the red and blue dresses that Patrice had picked out for them, as she said it went with the 4th of July "feel". Melody, always the dare-devil, chose to offset the girlish taste with a pair of converse sneakers, which was sure to piss off Patrice if she saw them.

Ashley on the other hand felt a new sense of glamor she had never been able to experience before. She took in all of the excitement and aspects that Melody hated.

"I just love this dress!" Ashley stated as she pulled at the bottom to show her shoes.

Melody rolled her eyes, "Look, I'm glad that you're feeling pretty and all, but don't forget the task at hand."

Ashley looked at the floor, and kept pace with Melody as they walked the floor and made sure to be seen but not heard.

"Hmmph, just once I want a normal day with her," Ashley whispered to herself.

The first hour seemed like an eternity as the girls claimed stake at the cushioned reading area in the drawing room.

Ashley picked up the *Canterbury Tales* by Chaucer that Robert had been perusing the night before, and got lost in the pages.

Melody was on the lookout for Patrice and Robert. She saw them schmoozing across the room, but Patrice noticed the converse, and mouthed an unintelligible statement to her while she attempted to keep her cool.

Melody redirected her eyes to the vaulted ceiling. The walls around the bookshelves and the ceilings were painted with a gold leaf, and the shimmers made the event feel fancy. The red and white balloons that surrounded the floors and walls, mixed with the large Uncle Sam ice sculpture, and collectively made the ordeal feel cheezy. She knew that someone was going to get reamed out for Patrice's impulse buys.

Melody watched as Robert placed a hand on his acquaintence's shoulder and chuckled a few last remarks as he made his way to the dining table in the back of the room. He picked up a champagne flute and tapped a fork hand to it; alerting everyone to redirect their eyes to him. Melody shook Ashley out of her book daze, and they stood up, *it's showtime*, she thought to herself.

Robert clanked the fork end to the champagne flute, and the noise faded to silence. His hair slicked back made him look every bit as debonair as he had hoped.

Melody caught a few ladies from the younger twenties crowd oggle him with their eyes, as they whispered to their friends and giggled. A crisp black suit covered every inch of him, as well as accentuated his slightly toned body.

Patrice stood next to him as she wore a long off white evening dress. It featured a slit up the thigh to showcase more of her body. Her hair was pinned up in a messy style bun that had strands fall around her face, and her pearl earrings were prominent against her blonde hair.

"Everybody, I'd like to make a toast, first to my wonderful wife, Patrice, for setting up this lovely soiree," He turned to her and placed his arm around her waist, drawing her closer, "Honey, you have done a fantastic job at throwing this together on short notice."

The room erupted in applause.

"Second, I'd like to make a toast to Dan Meltront. Without him, we wouldn't be here today, and we need to recognize the wonderful life he led."

Robert raised his glass in the air, and succinctly the rest of the room followed in line.

"To Dan!" The glasses were clinked together throughout the room, and champagne was gulped down in his honor.

"Oh gag me with a spoon," Melody snarled. Her mind was racing with finding the perfect time to interrupt his evening.

"We can still back out of this, Mel," Ashley said as she attempted to calm her friend down. Her pleas were ignored.

Robert began to start as Melody walked forward with the rainbow macrame purse in tow.

Chapter Twenty Five

Robert's voice echoed through the room, "It's been almost eight wonderful years with Patrice and—"

"Wonderful years, my ass!" Melody shouted.

She garnered gasps from around the room. Whispers infiltrated every corner, as they murmured presumably about the unruly daughter.

"These past eight years have been nothing but a living hell with you," Melody yelled as she placed her hands on her hips.

"Melody Meltront, you stop it this instant!" Patrice shrieked as she shoved her Jimmy Choo into the floor. "I will not have you talking to your father like that." Patrice started to walk toward Melody, before she stopped for a second to finish the sentiment, "...especially in front of all of our lovely guests!" she attempted to lighten the moment.

"And I will not have YOU claiming him as my father! My father died eight years ago at the hands of you two and I will not go one more day allowing you both to walk all over his grave, parading around his house, and calling everything HE did yours," she poked her finger into Robert's chest. "You're a disgrace to ever step foot in this house, claiming to be good enough to be my father!" Melody glared at Patrice.

Patrice walked closer and grabbed Melody swiftly by the arm, and she whispered in her ear with a smile on her face for the crowd, "You little brat. You better stop right now and retreat to your room with your little friend. After all that I've done for you."

Melody ripped herself away and walked to the head of the table, "After all you've done for me? What exactly have you done mother?"

The room paused and stared at Patrice who was busy fumbling with her words and pulling her dress down as it rode up.

"I..uh..um." Patrice's brain became more and more frazzled by the second as she attempted to save face for the guests.

"You've ridden the curtails of dad's money ever since you squandered your family's!"

Everybody was invested in what Melody had to say. Never had they seen such a display of gossip front and center. Phones were out, and guests recorded, as Patrice tried to block them and tell them it was all staged.

"And mom, since we're on the subject of dad...," She paused to face the crowd, "Exhibit one, I found this in Robert's office in a file under dad's name." Melody pulled out the small vial and pushed it into Robert's face, "Care to explain this?"

"Oh my lord, is that what I think it is?" a lady in the crowd murmured.

"It can't be," another gasped.

Ashley stood in the back corner with Bernie, neither of them not knowing quite what to do, but knew better than to step into a *family affair*. Merna, who hadn't heard any of the chaos, had begun to enter with hors d'oeuvres, but simply spun in a circle and re-entered the kitchen when she realized what was happening.

"I don't even know what that is, Melody," Robert cooly answered as if the circus around him was a charade.

"Arsenic, and from the looks of my research, it mimics every symptom dad experienced and can mirror cancer symptoms. Likely coincidence?," she folded her arms in front of her, "I think not. And another thing..." Melody began to go into her bag for the book just as Patrice rushed forward and she was stopped.

"Melody Ann, that vial was your father's medication," Patrice divulged. "It was *for* his cancer treatments," she pleaded as a way to get the crowd back on her side so that she could stop the gossip train from rolling to the public eye.

Robert walked to them and placed his hand on Melody's shoulder. Her skin crawled and her fingers curled in rage wanting to keep going, but she was trapped between them, and she risked losing the book for nothing. Instead, she clutched the bag, and listened to Robert.

"You see, your father was very ill, and one of the high risk treatments was the use of Trisenox, or as you would see from ingredients—arsenic. He was dosed in small amounts to combat the cancer cells, but not enough to ever poison him," His face looked at Melody's with a hint of remorse and sympathy, but the grip on her neck told her she was in for it later, "Your father wasn't murdered or whatever you have made up in your mind, and I do wish that one day you'll come to understand the circumstances, and begin to heal and accept me as your family."

Not a dry eye was in the house, except for those who lived in the manor. All dabbed their tears with tissue paper and applauded the family bonding moment from tragedy that had just witnessed. No longer did they see a potential for a crime, or a case of an unruly teenager, but more so they saw the sad story of a little girl who struggled with the death of her father.

Patrice and Robert were able to spin the story into their favor, and save face for another day. Patrice dug her nails into Melody's arm, and whispered through the side of her mouth, "Go to your room, now, and don't you dare come out until all the guests have gone."

Melody felt like she no longer had a platform to speak on, and chose to pick a battle for a different day. She walked back to the corner to get Ashley before they headed to their room to discuss a new plan.

Robert and Patrice held hands together at the front of the table once again ready to finish their speech.

"Now if I could finish my speech, I thought it would be best to tell everybody the news all at once before it becomes public knowledge. Patrice and I are planning to sell this manor come fall, as it sits unattended for long stretches of time. We have decided that the money would be better suited to go into our new charity we have created: Operation Shelter." Robert paused for applause.

"Thank you, thank you. We felt that this was more in line with what Dan would have wanted," Patrice inserted into the conversation as she offered a fake smile for the cameras.

"Operation Shelter will be raising funds to donate beds to those in need during the winter months of New York. It's—"

Melody felt every muscle in her body tense up with rage. Her fingers manipulated into different poses as she fought back the desire to run up and choke them. She gave one quick look at Ashley, who was mouthing the words *don't do it!*. But Melody did it and she was coming in hot.

"Are you fucking kidding me!"

"Watch your language young lady," shouted Patrice.

"I am over this, you are the worst human being. How could you sell dad's manor?" She ran at Patrice, but Patrice snapped her fingers and out of nowhere Bernie was there to hold her back as her legs kept going; running in place."How could you!"

The tears poured down her cheeks as she sobbed and Bernie lifted her up and carried her out in his arms.

Behind them, Melody could hear the sound of them as they finished their speech and the crowd clapped, but internally all she could feel was an intense hate, and a desire that grew to find a way out of there.

"Bernie, how could she do this?" Melody asked through shallow breaths. "How could she sell dad's home? The only place I can remember him by?"

"I don't know, Miss Melody. I don't know."

They stood in silence as Bernie held her close and rubbed her head. Ashley came up to them and took her friend's hand, and together they walked to their room, where Melody weeped until she fell asleep in Ashley's arms.

Chapter Twenty Six

July 4th

Dear Something or Other,

It's me again, Melody. I'm beginning to feel defeated.

Tonight, my mother decided to tell everyone that they're listing the manor for sale. Dad's manor. My happy place. All gone. What right does my mother have to sell this place? It was dad's, not hers.

Pushing through senior year is no longer going to be easy. She'll have officially gotten rid of everything that was one Dad's to make way for *his* stuff. Who even knows if I'll be able to get away from them at the end of the year.

I feel like I'm drowning at the bottom of the lake, feeling the torture of the water enter my lungs, while being held down by an invisible force.

I feel like I'm broken inside, and not one person understands. The wounds sliced deeper and deeper.

I feel like I'm done for now.

There's no hope to go on. Mysteries can solve themselves. Who would care anyway, right?

MM

Chapter Twenty Seven

The majority of July was spent by Melody giving up. She no longer wanted to get out of bed, and opted to have breakfast served in her room. Her hair was never brushed and Ashley couldn't get her to talk.

Ashley didn't recognize her friend anymore, as she had never known Melody to be defeated.

In the initial week, Ashley begged her to watch *Dexter* with her or to go out to town and do something, but Melody sat there in silence.

By the second week, Ashhley pulled Reed in to try to get her to come out by force. Together they attempted to grab her and drag her out of the room, but it was of no use as she just clung to the bed, and fought and screamed to be left alone.

Ashley spent most of her time with Reed in an effort to give Melody some space, but in truth, she missed her friend.

In the adult realm, Robert had begun to become quiet around the house since the party. He no longer challenged Melody, and Melody no longer went against him. Patrice, on the other hand, did not forget anything that was spoken that evening. Her mood turned for the worse, and daily she tasked Merna and Bernie with everything she needed and more—wearing them down hour by hour.

This allowed her to focus on Melody, as she prodded to find out how she knew about the squandering of her family's money. Melody never answered her, and to no avail she'd come in at least once a day to pry the information out of her, and much like Melody the point was moot.

Chapter Twenty Eight

July 16th

Dear Diary,

It's already the middle of July, and Melody refuses to come out of her room. She's been completely silent for almost two weeks now, and the only thing she does is eat and sleep.

And let me tell you one thing, spending the summer in a creepy manor with your friend is one thing, but spending it with a mute friend is another. I've felt on edge here without her banter between Patrice and Robert. There's no longer a case to solve because I can't stay awake long enough to hear the noise, and because Melody is at the point of no return and ready to throw in the towel to her life. I've never seen her so shattered, as if the manor was the piece that was holding her together.

On a positive note, I have been spending more time with Reed, due to the circumstances. I really enjoy spending time with him and getting to know him. He loves to crack dad jokes, and it makes me laugh. I actually almost had my drink come out of my nose on our....date (hehe!)...yesterday. He's just an all around wholesome person to be with.

I don't know what it is about him, but when we're together I'm able to forget about my anxiety and relax. We talk about books, and all the things that interest us. He feels like home to me, and I really needed that right now.

I know that Melody is my best friend forever and always, but I needed to expand my horizons with someone else and find who I am—not just who I am with Melody.

Here's to hoping Melody snaps out of it soon.

Sincerely,
Ashley

Chapter Twenty Nine

July 22nd

Dear Diary,

No update on Melody. She's still a sack of potatoes.

In Reed's World, things have been amazing! Yesterday, he texted me to meet him outside. He refused to tell me where we were going and we drove out of the swamplands and went to a peach orchard. Oh my lanta, the scenery was beautiful. I always knew Georgia was famous for peaches, but couldn't wrap my mind around the idea of peaches being anywhere near swamps. It was like a whole different state.

He ended up setting up a picnic, and we ate and laughed, and watched the clouds as they rolled by. And then it happened....

Diary, I got my first kiss! Completely unexpected, but I'm glad it happened all the same. It was lovely, honestly, and everything I could have dreamed of. My hand was in his and we laid there in silence identifying the clouds as pigs and dogs. Before I knew it he had rolled over and looked into my eyes with this brilliant smile. The ways his eyes twinkled. It felt like those cheesy Hallmark movies I love so much.

My heart can't stop doing flips, and I'm so happy—I just wish I could tell Melody all about it...maybe soon.

Sincerely
Ashley in Love

Chapter Thirty

July 22nd

Okay, enough with the formalities. You're just a piece of paper, not some magic end all cure to the way I've been feeling.

Is there a way to get this summer to end? If they're going to sell it, don't make me sit here and watch as buyers come and go to place bids, and don't make me remember the memories of these walls.

I know everybody thinks I should snap out of this, but I don't see that happening.

Every day, I watch as Ashley runs off to be with Reed. Maybe it's better this way. You know, lose everything at once so the pain can go away faster. She's probably over my weird habits, and my attitudes.

Who would blame her?

I can't find the strength to use my voice and talk, and I'm sorry for being a disappointment.

MM

Chapter Thirty One

It was nearing the end of July, which meant the girls were only there for a few more weeks of summer. Ashley had Reed come pick her up, and they went out to grab ice cream in town. The car ride was somber, and Ashley stared out at the trees that passed by.

Reed interrupted the deafening silence,"So, how's Melody been?"

"She's okay, I guess...," she turned to face Reed, "It's like she's a shell of who she used to be. I've never seen her like this, Reed."

"I remember my mom doing something similar when Melody's dad died. She didn't want to come out of the house for months. It took us telling her it was for something important to get her to come out, and once she was out she slowly came back to reality, " He twisted his lips to one side, "It was sad, really."

"That's how I feel watching her. I just want to shake her. She no longer wants to watch her mystery shows, and no longer wants to solve the mystery of what Robert's hiding in his office or what the sounds in the walls are."

"Have you heard anything at night since the last time?"

"No, I try. I really do. The thing is I can't keep my eyes open and I wake up in the morning only realizing that I fell asleep once again."

"And Melody, has she heard anything?"

"No," Ashley shook her head, "At least I don't think so. She's been going to sleep early every night while I read, and waking up in the afternoon. I don't even know if she'd care if she did hear it again." She picked at her nails, "Once she got hyperfocused on taking down Robert at the party, she stopped caring about the walls."

"Why don't I come over this weekend?"

"And do what? Melody's just going to sit there like a bump on a log."

"If she doesn't come around to anything we try, we can wait until everyone's asleep and you and I can stay up to listen for the sound again. Maybe if we hear it again, we can get her up to her old ways." He smiled and reached for Ashley's hand, "It's worth a shot at least!"

"She has never shied away from a mystery when it's dangled in front of her. Maybe this is just what the doctor ordered. Thanks, Reed". She leaned over as he drove, and placed a small kiss on his cheek.

Reed touched the spot, and smiled. His face grew redder by the minute. "It might be a good idea to tell her the news as well. I don't want it to hit her as another surprise...."

Ashley nodded her head in agreement, and held Reed's hand tighter as they pulled into the ice-cream shop parking lot.

Chapter Thirty Two

July 30fth

Dear Whoever

I think I'm finally coming to terms with the situation. I'm still not in a place to be around anyone—including Ashley—but I have decided to focus on things that I can change in my life. The biggest thing I've been thinking about is college. I want to make sure I have all my ducks in a row, though, before I bring it up to Ashley.

Lately, Ashley's been gone most of the day with Reed, and I don't think she knows that I know she's in love. Good for her though, he seems to make her happy, and as long as he makes her happy I won't have to step in and punch his face, ya know.

That's off topic though, and the real thing I wanted to get off my chest is college. I've spent the last month wondering where my life is going to go in the future. What would my dad say right now? What do I want to do for a job? Where do I see myself the happiest? The boring questions that Ashley would usually ask me.

After a lot of consideration, I think that I have settled on going to college for criminal justice. I really want to help people—which I think would make dad happy and also keep me humble.

Ashley would be shocked if she even knew I was entertaining the idea, but I think she would be most shocked that I created a pros and cons list. I never understood the point of those things, but man did it help me get my thoughts in one place.

Obviously, you can see that the pros outweigh the cons, and I had to just accept that I should try to go to college. Geesh, I'm starting to sound like Goon.

I hear her pulling back up, I better go. She might have me committed if she knew I was doing a diary like she suggested.

MM

August

Chapter Thirty Three

The weekend came after days of Ashley coaxing Melody to finally at least attend breakfast. No longer having challenging banter with Patrice nor Robert, Melody stayed in her seat, moving her fork around the food, and from time to time she'd actually take a bite.

"Melody, will you please stop this nonsense!" Patrice slammed her chardonnay onto the table.

"Your mother's right, Melody, it's really time to put on your big girl pants and deal with the inevitable. I know this place means a lot to you, but it's just sitting here gathering dust," Robert pleaded.

For the first time since she knew him, Ashley could tell that he was sincere. She wasn't sure what about, but there was something that troubled him, just as much as it bothered Melody. His hair was slightly disheveled, and began to grow to an unkempt length. His ties no longer matched his sweaters, and he no longer wanted to wear Melody down.

"Oh, who cares if it's because the place is gathering dust! I'd sell it just to be rid of it! There was nothing good in this manor, and it's time we truly begin our life back in New York," stated Patrice.

Ashley watched Melody. Her expression never waned as she took it all in, but said nothing.

"I give up with you," Patrice stood up at the table and slammed her hands on the table, "You've got one month left in this precious place of yours so I'd advise you to perk up and appreciate what little you have left!" She threw her napkin onto the table and left the room.

Robert stood up, "I better get on to check on her," he walked out of the room but stopped behind Melody's chair. He wanted to say something, but the words didn't want to come out. They were trapped in his throat, and he closed his mouth, offering a simple touch of the shoulder instead, "I'm sorry," he whispered and then he walked out.

Melody finally looked up from the plate and at the door turning on its hinge. She looked across the table to Ashley in confusion, and then went back to her plate.

What was that about? Ashley thought to herself. *Very strange...*

Chapter Thirty Four

"Bernie, bring in the decorations!" Patrice snapped her fingers and drew down her sunglasses as she stepped inside.

The girls came out from breakfast to Bernie stumbling in the doorway.

"Let me help you, Bernie, since *she* can't seem to have an inch of respect." Melody sneered.

"He's the help, Melody. It's his job. I'll never understand the way you and your father look at the world."

"Don't worry because we never understood why you're such a bitch," Melody shouted as she took some bags from Bernie's hands, and Ashley went to the car to fetch more. "You do realize that Bernie is a person,too, right?"

Patrice poised her nose to the air and sauntered off for her afternoon chardonnay.

"Miss Melody, please don't worry about me, I have this." Bernie said softly as he finally caught his breath.

"Bernie I care more about you than her, don't ever forget," she said as she hugged him.

Ashley finished bringing in the remaining bags. "What is all of this for?""Mrs. Drewmore has decided to throw one last soiree at the manor, before selling. She's hoping that a potential buying will come to view it." He lowered the bags onto the floor and bent backwards—cracking his back.

"She's not selling dad's manor, if I have any say," Melody threw her fist in her open palm.

"Well, Miss Melody, if you so desire to end her interest in selling, you better do it quickly."

"Why's that? We have at least a month left."

"No, Miss Melody. She's throwing the party next weekend, and then you all will be leaving two weeks early."

Melody grabbed Ashley by the arm, "Let's go, we have to crack this case, and time is ticking!"

"I think we have Melody back, Bernie!" Ashley squealed with delight as she was dragged up the stairwell.

"Have fun Miss Melody and Miss Ashley! I hope you crack the case!" Bernie shouted.

Melody paced the floor in the bedroom. "Okay, three weeks left. We can work with this."

"I'm just happy you're out of bed!" Ashley smiled.

"Goon, listen, we have no time to delay."

"Me, delay? Give yourself that peptalk Miss Dreary. You're the one who laid in your bed and barely talked to anybody for almost the past month!"

Melody stopped.

"I haven't been depressed nor dreary," she looked Ashley dead in the eyes, "I've been keeping myself from going off the deep end and wringing their necks. I've been telling myself 'no don't murder them and make it look like an accident. I've been–".

"All right, hold on right there Dexter Morgan. I don't want to hear any more incriminating ideas in case you actually do it," Ashley placed her hand into the air in a high-five position. "Besides, you need to get dressed in actual clothing instead of what you're wearing."

Melody looked down at her clothing to realize she was in a week-old sweater with egg and coffee stains. Her sweatpants that were once light blue now faded in areas to a dingy dark gray from not being cleaned. "I guess I have been lacking on my hygiene."

"That you have, and we need to get ready before Reed comes over."

"Reed? Why's he coming?"

"Originally, it was to get you out of your slump and get you back on the case of the mystery sounds."

"Back on the case?"

"Shush, you know exactly what I'm talking about."

Melody's mouth opened, but Ashley interrupted.

"Now that you're alive again, we can skip the hard work and get right into it!"

Ashley walked to the dressers and pulled out an outfit. She threw it at Melody who held it in her hands looking at the clothes before her, and then back to Ashley.

"When did you become so domineering?"

"Since you decided to take a break, someone had to step into those big bossy boots," Ashley smirked.

Melody smiled back and together they got ready to plan before Reed's arrival.

Chapter Thirty Five

The sun set in the swamplands, and the moon was itching to rise. Colors of pink and purple swirled in the misty air, as Reed pulled up to the mansion. He looked up to see the light on in the girls room, and surprisingly witnessed not one but two moving shadows.

Finally, he smiled.

He got out of his car, and walked up the steps to the door. After he knocked twice, he was coldly greeted by Patrice at the door.

"Who are you?" she sneered

"Um, we met last month, I'm a friend of Melody's. My name's Re—".

He was interrupted before he could finish his name.

"Listen, whoever you are. Make sure that you three stay out of my hair," she raised her right hand to her mouth, and poured the remainder of the chardonnay down her throat. "I'm tired of you all choosing to do whatever you please, and that brat wanting to make me the social pariah of the season."

She slipped in her heels and caught her balance on the frame of the door.

Reed had no idea what to say, but he nodded in agreement to slowly get by. "Yes, mam."

"They're up there," she mumbled as she pointed to the staircase and closed the door. "And be quiet, I have a migraine."

He walked to their bedroom, and walked into the bedroom, closing the door behind him. "What's up with your mom?"

Melody looked up from her seat on the floor. Her eyes looked confused. "Huh?"

"She looks like she's had a lot to drink. She slurring her words and calling you a brat because you ruined her life or something."

"That's just a typical night for Patrice," she said as she waved her hand for the next question.

Reed looked to Ashley who gave him a welcoming smile, "Aren't you glad to see Miss Gloom and Doom back in the game?"

"I can say I'm surprised," Reed joked.

"Ha. Ha.," Melody scoffed. "Let's get down to business shall we? How about we play what's in the padlocked room, one last time!" She cracked her knuckles and the sound made Ashley cringe.

"Ugh, I hate when you do that!" Ashley's shoulders were scrunched to her neck and her fingers manipulated into different poses.

"How can I help?" asked Reed.

"You're going to go with us. That passageway is dark in the day time, it's going to be worse at night. One of us is going to have to decide who goes first."

"Nose goes!" yelled Ashley as she put her finger on her nose.

Melody came in second.

Reed was last.

"Damn it, I will never win that game," he pushed back his hair, and Ashley bit her lower lip looking at him.

Melody was eyeing the two of them up. Her eyes darted back and forth between them. "Is there something you two need to tell me?"

"Um, nope," replied Ashley.

Reed looked at Ashley for support as Melody honed her eyes on him.

"Anything Reed....?" Melody drew out her words which caused anxiety to build up in him.

Reed's eyes scanned the floor in an attempt to not lock eyes again.

"Reed."

"Ashley, come on! She scares me!" Reed stammered.

"Oh, geez fine!. Yes, while you were comatose in your bed, I had nothing better to do than to go to town all the time," Ashley pressed her fingers together at her sides, "Well, I got to hang out with Reed a lot more, and we ended up having a lot in common."

"And?"

"And, well, we ended up going out on a date...and maybe we're more than friends now," Ashley's eyes grew with fear of not knowing what her best friend would say.

Melody jumped, and ran up to them. She placed one arm around each of their shoulders and gave them a pat on the back.

"That's fantastic, I always told you that you two were flirting that first day!"

Reed facepalmed, and Ashley was shocked at how well Melody was handing it. *Maybe she's manic.*

"All right, you two love birds, how about we crack a case, save a manor, and get you two back in time for another date before we leave?"

"She's definitely acting weird," Ashley whispered to Reed.

"She's *always* acting weird, I told you she scares the living daylights out of me," he replied back.

"Let's map out our plan. Reed you get to hold this handy dandy flashlight and lead the way. Ashley, you take the rear, so that you can have a fast exit if need be."

"Thanks, Mel," she said sarcastically.

"Once we make an advancement on the door, we should be able to use the skeleton key to get in there." She closed her notebook, and looked at the two of them, "Sound like a plan?"

"Sounds good," they chimed in unison.

"When should we go?" Reed questioned.

"Let's wait until everybody's in bed, and give it a few hours to see if the noise appears first. I want to see if the sound is traveling or in the room itself when we go down there."

Melody clapped her hands together. "And now we wait," her index finger pointed in the air.

The three of them attempted game after game to wait out the adults. The hours seemed long and arduous as they had few means to occupy themselves quietly. Rounds of tic-tac-toe followed by solitary and even a round of Clue to get them in the mood.

Each fought to stay awake, as they heard Patrice downstairs pour glass after glass of wine and shout through the manor.

"When will she stop?" Ashley moaned as her eyes slowly closed.

"When the alcohol runs out," Melody yawned.

"I feel bad for that liver," Reed grimaced.

"Liver? What liver?" Melody rolled her eyes.

They looked over at Ashley who was now fast asleep on the floor. Melody stretched her arms, and grabbed three pillows from the bed. She placed one under Ashley's head, and threw one at Reed.

"We might as well get some sleep while we wait for *that* to quiet down," Melody pointed her head towards the door.

"Sounds good to me."

All three of them were sprawled on the floor, while they waited for the hours to tick by.

CREEEEEAK!

CREEEEEAK!

No one heard the first few sounds of the rattling in the walls.

CREEEEEAK!

"Help me," came a small voice through the cracks, "Please!"

Reed opened his eyes first. He looked around the room and saw nothing but shadows and the casting of the moonlight on the walls. He rubbed his eyes, and started to go back to sleep.

CREEEEEAK!

"HELP!"

This time it sounded closer, and it jostled Reed awake.

He shook each girl, "Hurry! I hear the sounds!"

"Melody, please, I don't want to look at blood patterns!" Ashley's drool pooled on the floorboards.

"Ashley, it's Reed, wake up! Someone's calling for help!"

"Give her a second, she'll snap out of it," Melody said as she wiped her face with her hand to wake herself up.

Melody got off of the floor and walked to Ashley. She grabbed her by the feet and dragged her across the boards. "Wake up, goon!"

Ashley moaned from sleep depravation, and Reed shook his head, "You two have a weird relationship."

"That we do," said Melody as she dropped Ashley's legs.

Slowly Ashley rose off the ground and dusted herself off. "You didn't have to do that," she whispered.

"Help me!" The three of them heard the pleas for help.

"Is that Patrice calling for help?" Ashley questioned.

Melody tiptoed across the hall and peered in at the two sleeping bodies. Four feet dangled from the bed's edges and she knew it couldn't be them.

"Please," the whisper came again.

Reed moved closer to the brick wall in the room. A small black fireplace was on the wall, it hadn't been used in years, and Reed stepped back at the sight of a spider's web that was on the corner. "I hate those things," he muttered.

He moved closer the sounds on the walls grew louder, and he beckoned for the girls to come listen. They placed their ears up against the wall and waited again.

CREEEEAK!

Ashley pointed to the large crack in the wall. Melody squinted and walked to it, glancing through the slight sliver. In it she could barely make out anything, and everything seemed black. She pulled away when she saw the blackness move before her eyes, and she fell back onto the floor.

"Help me!"

"Th...There's someone there!" she whispered, while her finger pointed at the crack.

"Are you sure it was a person?" Reed asked.

"I think I know what I saw!"

"Maybe it's a ghost!" Ashley held her arms to her chest and shivered.

"To the passageway!" Melody alerted them and off she went.

The three of them were off, following Melody, but each wanted to shrink back from fear.

Reed wondered why someone would be in the walls.

Ashley wondered if they were even alive.

Chapter Thirty Six

The moonlight shined overhead through the skylight of the foyer. Darkness filled every corner, and it was hard to see anything more than three feet in front of them. The three friends went to the secret passageway and touched the lion's head opening the door. The sound filled the house as the door slid open, and they paused and waited to see if either adult woke from their drunken slumber.

Melody gently slid the door back into place, and together they made their way to the wooden door.

"This scares me more at night," she crossed her arms and held herself

Reed came from behind and held her in his arms, kissing the top of her head. "It'll be okay," he whispered in her ear. He hugged her tighter, "I'm here, tonight."

Ashley smiled.

"Yea, and you're going first remember," Melody chimed in—ruining the butterfly effect in Ashley's stomach,

Ashley let out a sigh. "Let's get this over with." She took the flashlight and hit it in her palm to jiggle the batteries back to life. "Darn thing takes forever to turn on!"

Reed grabbed it from her hands and opened the door. He inhaled one last deep breath to gather his nerves and he ascended the stairs.

"Be nice to strangers, mom says. Yea, and look where that got me," he joked.

"Oh, you enjoy our company," Melody patted Reed's back.

They climbed the steps in the stone stairwell. The wall felt cold but wet with condensation from the outside heat.

Ashley's finger trailed the way up and she felt an eerie sensation. "I don't think we should be here," she said softly.

"Help me!" the moaning came from right in front of them.

Reed shined his light up the staircase, but saw nothing before them. "Where is it coming from?" he mouthed.

Melody looked back at Ashley with concern, Ashley's eyes grew with fear by the second, and her breathing became shallow.

"Just breath," Ashley said to herself. *In and out. In and out.*

"Please, help," the sound came again.

"Go up further!" Melody motioned for him to continue.

"I'm not doing it!" Reed said as he placed his hands in the air. The flashlight's beam shining on the ceiling

"Here give me that," Melody took the flashlight from Reed and barged past him.

The sounds of her footsteps echoed through the cavernous walls. She got to the locked room and pulled out her skeleton key. Melody placed it inside the hole and maneuvered it about until it released.

Just as she did, the register next to her feet moved. Melody moved the light to see what it was, and she was met with the register falling to the floor.

"Somebody's in there," she pointed at the room.

Melody made a countdown with her fingers: one...two...three...

She pushed with all her might to open the jammed door and stumbled into the dark room. Reed and Ashley looked for the lightswitch on the wall. Around them they heard the mysterious creaking sounds that plagued their summer. A figure began to emerge and shuffle in the darkness around them.

"Wh-Who is that?" Ashley managed to get out.

Melody moved her light around, but kept catching only glimpses of the figure. The sound of chains clattered on the floors.

"I found the light!" Reed shouted.

The light turned on, and each turned their head in a different direction in an attempt to find the suspect.

Ashley saw them first.

"Ahhhh!" she jumped back in fright.

Reed and Melody looked in her direction. "Oh my God," Melody mustered out.

Cowered in a corner was a woman with blonde hair and brown roots. Her face hidden behind a poster board dingy twin bed and a silver shackle tied to her wrist.

"Please, don't hurt me!," she said as she shielded herself with her arm—making an 'x' formation.

"We're not going to hurt you, m'am," Reed said as he stepped forward, "We're here to he–"

"No! Get away, don't hurt me!" she yelled.

Reed tensed up and backed away. He glanced at Melody who stepped forward.

"Can you tell me your name?" she asked sympathetically.

The woman cried into her hands. She sobbed and was losing the little voice she had left.

"My name is...My name is Mara," she managed to get out before she cried again.

Ashley grabbed Melody's hand, "Is that who I think it is?"

Melody nodded yes, and observed Reed's confused expression, "She's Robert's teaching assistant," she responded, "Mara's been missing since last year."

The woman attempted to wipe away her tears, but more came in their place. Ashley walked to her and let out a hand for Mara.

Mara's hands shook. She didn't know if she could trust these three teens.

"You can trust us," Ashley smiled at her. Mara's hand felt cold in Ashley's and when she stood up the shackles collided with the floor.

"Now we know where the sound came from," said Melody.

Mara walked to her bed and sat down; her body twitched at every movement.

The room was small, only about ten feet each way. A bed was pushed against one wall, a wooden antique wardrobe on another, and the other two contained a doorway—one that entered from the stairwell, and one that entered from the hallway next to Robert's office.

Dinner plates were piled under the bed, and flies fought to eat the scraps. Peeking out from below the wardrobe was a silver metal bed pan, filled to the brim with urine and feces.

"What happened?" Melody inquired.

"Melody, we need to get her help!" Reed reasoned.

"I can't help her, unless I know what happened."

Mara's eyes were like a deer in a headlight. She couldn't keep her eyes on someone for long as they darted around the room.

"How long did you say I was missing for," Mara asked. Her voice turned into a whisper.

"According to the newspapers, you disappeared at the beginning of the school year, which is almost one year ago," replied Melody.

Mara punched the wall, causing blood to drip out of her wounded knuckles, "How could he do this to me!" Her voice grew louder but the words came out dry and raspy.

"He?" asked Ashley.

"Robert! That bastard tells me he's going to get me out of here. That he's going to let me go," she sobbed again.

"That register over there, is that how you got out of this room?" Melody pointed back towards the doorway.

Mara shook her head yes, "He has me shackled so I can't get very far. I was so happy to get near your room, and when I noticed the crack I tried everything to get you to hear me!" Mara pulled at her chains, "I want these off!"

Ashley noticed her bruised wrists. "Oh, you poor woman!"

"We have to call the cops!" Reed was pacing the floor, trying to keep himself together. He pushed his hand through his black hair.

"If he finds me out of this room he'll kill me!" Mara burst into tears again.

On the other side of the door Melody noticed that the hallway light turned on.

"Hurry! Run, he's coming!" Melody started pushing Reed and Ashley to the door. She flicked off the lightswitch, before she paused, "We're going to come back for you!".

"Please, don't leave me!" Mara begged, her hand reached to her for support.

Melody ignored her pleas and managed to shut the door behind her and place the lock back on before she heard the door open on the other side.

"Who was in here with you?" Robert shouted.

"No one! I'm here by myself."

The handle on Melody's side jiggled and Melody ran towards the exit to the foyer with Reed and Ashley following close behind.

They reached the lion's head and slid the slightly cracked door back open, peering out to make sure Robert wasn't near. Each squeezed through, as Melody pushed the door back into its place.

There was no time to catch their breath as they ran up the steps, making sure not to make a sound for Robert to hear. At the top, they heard the door below them shut and the lock was placed back on. The pitter-patter of Robert's shoes filled the air as he made his way up the staircase.

"Go!" Melody mouthed to them, and they hastened their step.

Once they were in the room, the girls quickly got into bed as Reed lay on the pillows on the floor. Ashley turned away from the doorway and attempted to catch her breath. Her anxiety built up inside her and her airway tightening up.

All was silent.

No one dared to make a sound as the pitter-patter grew closer and closer with each second.

Reed closed his eyes.

Melody held her breath.

The door to the room creaked open, and in stepped Robert. His hair disheveled and his tie halfway off. He walked around the room, listening for any sound to show they were awake. As he passed each one he paused to look at their eyes, and watch as their eyeballs darted back and forth under their eyelids, sweeping for dreams.

He walked out of the room and closed the door behind him, and the girls and Reed waited until they heard him close his bedroom door.

Collectively, they let out their breath, and dared not to speak a word, but they all thought the same thing: *Am I still dreaming?*

Chapter Thirty Seven

"Merna!" shouted Patrice from downstairs, "I told you this house needs to be spotless!"

"Yes, m'am. Sorry, m'am," Merna apologized.

Melody got up and walked to Reed. "Come on get up," she said as she gently nudged him with her foot.

"Hey, goon, get up!" Melody said to Ashley, tossing a pillow onto her.

"Ughh, is it morning already?" Her hair was frazzled all around her and Reed laughed at the sight.

"Good morning, sleepyhead," he snickered with a smile.

Melody closed the door all the way. "Do any of you remember last night?"

The look in their eyes told each other what happened was real. A woman in a hidden room, kept from the world. But which one did it?

"All right, so are we all at the conclusion that it was Robert that locked her in there?" Reed asked first.

"Well who else would it be? Patrice? The woman can't even lock away the alcohol let alone an entire person." Melody was over Patrice's choices, and the more she grew older, the more she despised her mother, and never wanted to turn out like her.

"But she does have a motive, Mel," Ashley quipped.

"Weigh out the motives though, Robert was caught in a love affair that Mara didn't want to end. Patrice is just a jealous wife who wants to save face for the press."

"That's true," Ashley agreed.

"I still think we need to call the cops," Reed interrupted.

Melody walked to the window and peered down onto the driveway. Below Bernie was rushing from the car, while Patrice shouted orders at him. Her finger raised and pointed from the car to the house, and finally to Bernie as she told him he was incompetent. Melody turned back to her friends, "No, no cops. We need to get her out of here undetected. Who knows what Robert's capable of. And Patrice...well she'll do anything to keep it out of the press. *Anything.*"

"Anything? Do you really think anything she could do would be as evil as Robert keeping her chained to a wall? It's not like she's capable of murd–" Ashley tried to reason.

Melody stopped her, "I'm telling you when the woman doesn't want the press to know she might be able to pay someone to do her dirty work for her, Ash," she sat down on the floor and crossed her legs. "We'll be able to move her from the room during the party this weekend. They'll be too busy to notice, and we can sneak her out to Reed's car and get away."

"My car?"

"Your car. Neither of us have one, so you're going to be the hero, Reed. Isn't that lovely?" Melody chided.

Downstairs a loud clash filled the air as all of the silver dishes Merna was holding came tumbling to the ground. "God dammit, Merna," Patrice shouted, "Why do I have help if they can't even do the simple things I expect of them?"

The trio walked to the top of the stairs, "Mother, will you stop berating Merna and Bernie! They can't help that you don't know how to do anything for yourself, but that you insist on buying all of this crap for a party. Why don't you get off of your ass and lift a finger!"

"I beg your pardon, young lady? You will respect me, or else."

"Or else what?"

"Or else you and your little friend can stay up stairs tonight while one of Robert's business associates comes to look at the house," Patrice's red lipstick paired well with her sinister smile. She knew she had one this round, and Melody was going to be furious.

"Tonight?" Melody shrieked.

"Tonight," Patrice said poignantly. "And if all goes well, he will want to be sent the contract by the weekend, and we will cancel the party and leave this shithole to return back to New York," she said as she waved her hand at the manor, "I am over seeing this place, it's wretched and I don't know what charm your father ever saw in keeping this."

"Uh-oh," Reed let out by accident.

"Mel, keep calm. It's all going to be alright," Ashley said.

"Oh, it's going to be alright. Everything's going to be alright," Melody remarked.

"This isn't going to be good," Ashley shook her head.

The remainder of the day was spent watching Merna and Bernie rush to complete orders in time for the arrival of the dinner guest.

Robert was in his office, 'tending to things' as he put it, and Patrice was in the sitting room with bottles of chardonnay and wine. Her eyes were filled with a new emotion as she plotted ways to get out of Clinch county sooner than later. And with each sip of wine, she knew more and more of what needed to be done.

At seven on the dot, a blue '65 Thunderbird pulled in. The girls and Reed were in the garden mapping out a way to lead Mara to freedom.

"So if we just lead her from the passageway during the party, we can bring her out through the servant's quarters," Melody started.

"Then should we be bold and go through the front door?" Reed opposed.

"Of course not, nitwit. We make a left. There's a small door near the west wing, it leads to a storage space where Patrice used to put all of her out of date furniture. In the back there's a way to get outside," Melody pointed towards a small door blocked by the growing ivy on the wall of the manor.

"Where did that door come from?" asked Ashley.

Melody ignored her, "Anywho, we'll bring her out of there, and–"

"Hi, there all you young folk," a charming man of possibly his mid forties approached the group. His hair was red, with streaks of gray throughout. He wore glasses and his smile was nearly perfect. "Mr. Raust," he said as he reached out his hand. "Nice glasses, by the way, young lady," he pointed towards Ashley's rims that were eerily similar to hers.

"Nice to meet you," Ashley said as she went to shake his hand.

Melody struck her hand down, "Sorry, we don't talk to old strangers."

"Oh, but I'm not a stranger, I know your father, Robert," he smiled.

"That's not my father, and you're still a stranger," she expressed, "Let's go guys," Ashley and Reed followed her back into the manor, as Mr. Raust walked to the front door with a shrug of the shoulders. A briefcase swung in his hand, and he knocked.

"Oh, Charles, lovely to see you dahrling!" Patrice greeted him with a hug with her right arm, and a glass in hand on the right.

"Patrice, great to see you again as well. It's been ages since Robert's invited anybody over for a meal."

Inside they went as Patrice yelled for Robert. "I do hope you liked the outside view of this place," her hand touching his shoulder.

"Very Tudor style with an exquisite garden. The blooms for this time of year are my favorite."

"Oh, yea, I bet," Patrice feigned interest, "Robert!" she yelled.

Mr. Raust held his ear to fade out her voice.

"Yes, my love," Robert called from the hallway as he walked toward them. "Oh Charlie, old sport. Great to see you," he jogged to shake hands.

Melody listened from the top of the staircase, making sure to stay just out of sight.

"Patrice has just been showing me this place. Definitely something I'd be interested in to add to my portfolio. Care to take me around and show me the rest?"

"Have fun you two," Patrice waved them off as she downed the rest of the glass.

Robert and Mr. Raust walked in the direction of the kitchen. Melody couldn't hear them anymore, but could still see their expressions as Mr. Raust slapped Robert on the back as he laughed. She watched them as they rounded the corner, and then walked back to her room.

"Those arrogant jackasses."

"Does it seem like he's going to buy?" Ashley asked.

Melody's eye twitched, "...yes," she inhaled and let out a large breath of air, "but we still have time to stop it."

"And just how do you realistically plan to do that?" Reed questioned.

"I'm not sure..." Melody found herself uncertain again, but knew she had to try everything in her power to save the manor, "If we can rescue Mara, it'll at least delay the sale when she testifies to the cops," she put her fingers to her chin, "Perhaps it would even deter Mr. Whatshisface, because who would want a place with a bad rap?"

Ashley's lips curled to one side and she nodded in agreement, "It does sound like it would work," she glanced over at Reed, "It's going to suck leaving early now though.."

Reed put his hand over hers, "Don't worry. Hey, you know what, maybe I could come visit you both in New York!"

"Ohhh, great," Melody joked.

Ashley threw a pillow at her, "Stop it, I think it's a wonderful idea!" She slowly went over all of the things that they could do when he'd come.

Melody drowned out their voices, as she thought about all the memories that could potentially be lost with the manor. The ones of her father cooking and bringing waffles at three in the morning just to make her bad days better, and how they'd play hide and seek in all of the little pocket spaces of the place. The manor was where she grew up, and the place she called home. It made her feel warm and fuzzy–a feeling she no longer liked to feel. She placed her hand on the window pane. *I wish you were here with me Dad, you'd know what to do in every situation. You'd know the best way to get Mara out of here undetected and to safety. I'm not brave like you.*

Reed and Ashley came up behind her and hugged her. "Ewww get off me with the lovey dovey emotions!"

"Mel, if your father were here he'd say you were the bravest person he knows, we can do this *together,*" Ashley hugged her tighter.

Melody couldn't push it away anymore as she turned to face them and let them squeeze away the sadness. She closed her eyes for a moment, taking it all in. The smell of Ashley's hair wafting to her nostrils. *I love the smell of strawberries*, she thought to herself. It felt like an eternity before she opened her eyes, and when she did a large envelope slid under the door.

Chapter Thirty Eight

Melody pushed Ashley and Reed out of the way, and rushed to the door. Quickly she opened the door to see if she could see who left the envelope, but no one was in sight. She turned around with wild eyes, as she held it in her hands.

"What's that?" Ashley asked as her pointer finger dug into her thumb, "I hope it's not something terrible. I can't take it anymore."

Melody opened the yellow mystery and pulled out a stack of papers. "It must be more about dad," she fingered through the pages and saw many lines crossed out with black tape. "That's weird, it says it's from Blackwell Sanitarium."

"Sanitarium?" Reed stepped forward to look for himself.

"When did your dad go to an asylum, Mel?"

"He didn't," Melody confessed.

"It says here this is for a Ms. Patricia Lauxmont," Reed read out loud, "On July 1st, 1994 a Ms. Lauxmont was released from Blackwell

Sanitarium. She was found to be stabilized with medication for her bipolar disorder."

"Is there anything else?" Melody grabbed the papers out of his hands. "Ms. Lauxmont, admitted March 17th, 1993, after attempted homicide on the Lauxmont family's nanny. Ms. Lauxmont has confessed to stabbing the nanny repeatedly for what she says is "retribution for the disgrace of their family name". Ms. Lauxmont was found by her father while committing the crime, and he states she had found out about his marital affair with the young woman. Ms. Lauxmont will spend a one-year minimum to evaluate and assess for treatment according to court orders, in exchange for no jail time."

"Holy hell, your mother's a psycho!" Reed shouted.

"Shh, keep your voice down, you don't want her to hear you, you idiot." Melody placed her finger to her mouth. Listening to make sure nobody was coming, she started talking, "That explains why she hates the help so much."

Ashley pondered, "You know, I read somewhere, that in psychological conflict a person's traumatic events when they're younger can damage them as they age. Your mother probably reflects back on the affair and projects that all others in the position are like that."

Melody paced the floor, and tossed the packet of pages onto the bed, "No kidding, Sherlock," she mocked. "What I want to know is how did I never hear of this before? I'm sure dad didn't know, he wouldn't have married her, if so."

Reed picked up the papers, "Maybe, she hid it. There are a lot of black marks in this file that probably says a lot more condemning stuff. I'm sure her family paid them off like they probably paid off the nanny."

"That makes sense!" Melody snapped her fingers, and stopped pacing for a moment, "She does have a tendency to pay off people to keep hush, she had to have learned it from somewhere."

"Hey, what's this?" Reed picked up a small piece of paper, on it was a write-up of some sort. "Looks here that your mom got into trouble while there. It says she stole four vials of arsenic. She was caught trying to put it into the worker's food,"

"That must be where she got the arsenic from," Melody observed.

"Sounds like it...wait, no she couldn't have. It says here they were able to retrieve the three remaining vials. She confessed to using the contents of the fourth to try to poison the guard, and they found an empty bottle."

"It can't be that coincidental. She had to have planned something," Melody proclaimed, "When there's a will, there's a way with that woman, and she most likely found the way."

Knock, knock.

Ashley lunged for the papers and hastened to put them under the mattress, just as the door slowly opened.

"Knock, knock, children, Mr. Raust is leaving now. You ought to be good children, and go wish him goodbye, it's the least you could do since he's going to buy the manor," Patrice said as she smirked at Melody.

"He hasn't signed the contract, so it's not his yet," Melody pointed out, "And I refuse to say goodbye to any acquaintances of yours," she said as she crossed her arms.

"Oh, you will go down there," Patrice grabbed Melody's face," And you will be a good girl, and do as you are told, or else there will be consequences."

Patrice's red fingernails pressed into Melody's cheeks. They were puffed out from the compression, and she could no longer vocalize her words. Melody nodded in agreement as she succumbed to the fact that she would need to do it this once.

They walked down the stairs and into the sitting room, Mr. Raust saw them and stood up, "Oh, look at the lovely family, here." He looked at Melody with a sour expression, "This one here has a temper," he stated.

Melody was turning red in the face. Not from embarrassment this time, but from anger boiling inside of her. She didn't want to do as she was told, and she didn't want to allow this man the opportunity to buy the manor.

Patrice glared at her to say goodbye, politely. Melody walked up to Mr. Raust and extended her hand out. "I would just like to say..."

Mr. Raust extended his hand to shake, just as Melody finished her statement. She drew her hand into a fist, "...ef you," as she pointed her middle finger at him."

"Oh my heavens, Melody Ann Meltront. How dare you show that to our humble guest!" Her shrill screams filled the airways.

Bernie chuckled in the corner, and Patrice put him back into his place with her scolding stare.

"Haha. It's all right Patrice. She's just a little spitfire, ain't she?" He picked up his briefcase off the floor and walked to the door. "I should be back here by the middle of next week to finalize the papers. I hope you all bid well till then!"

Patrice was busy sending Mr. Raust off while Reed, Ashley, and Melody made their way back upstairs. She closed the door just as they got to the top, and looked back at Bernie. "You're fired!"

"Mrs. Drewmore, please, no!" Bernie pleaded as Patrice berated him for laughing at the situation.

"I will not tolerate any more insubordination in this house. That brat already undermines me, and I will not have the staff doing it as well," she snapped.

Melody ran down the stairs and stood in front of Bernie, "You can't fire Bernie! He's been with this place for decades!"

"I will do whatever I want. And after next week we won't need his help anymore. I want you packed and ready to leave by the time dinner's served. Oh, and I want that boy gone, too" And with that, she stormed off leaving Melody to hug a weeping Bernie.

"It'll be okay, Berns, I'll find a way to get you back here," Melody attempted to comfort him.

Bernie wiped away his tears, "What am I going to do?" He walked away and gathered his miscellaneous items around the house.

Melody looked at Reed and Ashley, who were holding hands. Their knuckles turned white as Ashley squeezed them.

"Well, I guess that's my cue to exit," Reed said, pointing toward the door. "Text me when you figure out what to do about you know what. We need to do it fast."

"I know, and from the looks of it, time's running out for everybody," Melody muttered as she pressed her hand against her eye and wiped it down her face. "I'm in over my head."

Ashley bit her lower lip, *This isn't good*, she thought to herself. *Melody never believes anything is too much. We're in trouble.*

Chapter Thirty Nine

The girls stepped outside to get fresh air into their lungs. Melody was feeling trapped inside the manor and became discouraged by the status of the situation at hand. She had already solved the mystery that she had set out to do, and now the new task was to find a way to get Mara to safety. But how does one get someone to safety, when they feel like they are drowning from the pressure?

Ashley touched her hand to a rose, and her fingers gently pressed the flowers as she felt their soft texture. She picked it off the vine and smelled it, *Mom's shampoo. I miss home*, she thought.

"Do you think it's time to just give up on the manor, Mel?" Ashley asked softly.

Melody whipped her head around, "How could you say that?"

Ashley's eyes grew concerned, and she wondered how to say her thoughts in a way that wouldn't make Melody defensive. They sat in silence for a few moments, while she gathered her words. "I know that this place reminds you of your dad, but like all things in life, there comes a point where we just have to move on. He wouldn't want you to be upset over this," she reached for Melody's hand for comfort.

Melody pulled her hand away and went to sit on the wooden swing. She pulled her legs up onto the boards and held her knees to her face. Looking around it was nothing but beautiful flowers surrounding the walls of the dreary stone manor. The manor was beautiful in its own way. The stones pieced together in a way that was seamless, and the trees edged the driveway just right that it made seeing the manor upon arrival look spectacular.

She felt like the manor was part of her identity. A place where she could feel the presence of her father, and keep his memory alive. A place away from Patrice and *him*. The manor was a sanctuary that she wanted to have forever, and hoped to one day take control of.

"I don't think I *can* let go," Melody answered.

Ashley sat down on the swing and placed Melody's legs across her lap. "I *know* you can. You're braver than you think," she paused, "Just let this go, and focus on how to help Mara. We can save her...you can save her."

They sat there swinging in silence.

"Aren't you ever scared of the unknown?" Melody questioned. "Aren't you ever wondering what if you go forward and something comes out of nowhere like a curveball ready to slam you in the face?"

"Like any idea or plan, I always outweigh my pros and cons. Sometimes I can back it up with research, but there are times where you just have to freefall into the abyss and take it as it comes. You can't know everything about the future, it would make life banal,"

"I get it, but please stop with the Encyclopedia Brown stuff," Melody's face was serious, "*banal*", she said as she busted out laughing. Melody composed herself, and her face scrunched up, "But what do

I do about that *thing?* I think she definitely had a motive to kill dad, and the story in the chart doesn't add up. What if she kept the vial for all of those years, and used it on dad?"

Ashley put her hands on Melody's legs, "Mel, I can't help you fix crazy, but I always like to think that what goes around comes around for everyone, and she'll get her comeuppance."

The night air came in and the fog from the nearby swamps came in routinely. The sun was setting on one side, while the moon rose on the other, and the colors of the sky resembled a healing bruise.

Melody took a deep breath in through her nose, and slowly exhaled through her mouth. "I just have to keep reminding myself that I have only one year left. I have to get through one more year," she held Ashley's hand, "And I've settled, I'm attending university with you. It's not my dream, but it'll do and I'll have you by my side."

Ashley smiled, and squeezed Melody's hand, "You have no idea how happy that makes me, Mel!"

"I guess, we could even, like, I don't know get our own dorm together...or something...," Melody said nonchalantly.

"Ooo, really?? We could have small plants in the window, and get matching bed sets!"

Ashley listed every fun thing she planned to do to their room, while Melody took it all in. *One year, I can make it.*

"Girls! Come in, dinner's ready!" Patrice shouted from the front doorstep.

"Dinner?" Ashley asked, "I figured she would have fired Merna like she did Bernie."

"She could never," Melody rolled her eyes, "That woman doesn't even know how to boil an egg. We'd be living off of takeout food if she fired Merna."

Ashley nodded in agreement, "Good point there." And together they walked into the manor.

They hit the front door step, and immediately smelled the aroma of a roast.

"Mmm, Merna's cooking smells delicious," Ashley licked her lips.

"Get along girls, before dinner gets cold," Patrice shouted from the dining room.

They entered just as Merna was placing the remaining sides on the table. The white table cloth had large bowls of salad on each end, serving dishes of brussel sprouts, and large candles lit to set the tone of the room.

The flickering of the candles on the wall created an eerie presence of dancing shadows, and at each end was Patrice and Robert. Robert wore a blue sweater over a brown dress shirt, his face half dimmed. Patrice on the other hand opted for a more radiant look as she appeared in a silver glittering cocktail dress. Her hair was styled into a crimp, and to Ashley she looked like a modern take of a flapper girl.

Once the girls were seated, Merna bowed slightly and stepped back as Patrice stabbed the meat from the serving tray.

"After today's events, I've come to realize that we have only days left in this dreadful place," Patrice put the tray down, and Merna picked it up to carry to the girls, "And with the news of our impending departure, we know that we will no longer need help around here."

Merna stood at the wall. Her body slightly shook from nerves at what Patrice was about to say.

"Since we won't be owning this place anymore, I've begun the process this morning of firing the help. This morning it was Bernie," Patrice finished putting her plate together, and then looked up at Merna, "And now it's you. I'm sorry, but after this meal we will no longer be needing your service either."

Merna sobbed, “Mrs. Drewmore, please, I have a family!”

“I’m sorry, Merna, I truly am, but there is no need to have help on a payroll if there is no home for them to be helped in. Here, let me help ease the pain,” Patrice pulled out her checkerboard, and wrote a check, “A check. For you. It's $5,000, quite a large sum for you, I know I'm generous.” She passed the check to the edge of the table, and Merna grabbed it with tears running down her face. “You know what, I think you can go now, actually,” she said grinning as she glanced around the table.

Merna ran out of the room crying.

“Why are you doing this!” Melody screamed.

“Because I can,” Patrice sneered, “I have the money and I have the control.”

“Money doesn’t give you the power to be miserable.”

“No, but it does allow me to do as I please,” Patrice dug into her plate and cut up her vegetables into small palatable pieces.

“Now, Melody. This place is your mother’s, and you need to learn to live under her rules until you’re 18 and hopefully on your own,” Robert interjected as he picked up his cup of coffee from the table to ingest while reading the evening paper, not once looking up.

“Blah, blah, blah. That’s all I ever hear from both of you!” Melody listened as she heard the sound of the front door shut and Merna getting into her car. “I’m sick and tired of you always acting as if I don’t have a say.”

Ashley clutched her stomach, “Mel, I don’t feel so good.”

“What’s wrong, Ash?”

The look in Ashley’s eyes grew fearful, “I feel like I”m going to pass out. My head...it’s....I’m,” Ashley could barely stammer out her words, “Everything is fuzzy,” she said as she held her head in her hands.

"Do something!" Melody stood up and shouted at Patrice, who simply looked back at her with a smile. She turned her attention to Robert for help, "Please, help her!" she pleaded as Ashley's head hit the table and she was out cold.

"Oh my," Robert said with a worried face, "Patrice, dear get up, somethings wrong—" Robert's legs bowed as he tried to walk. Soon he was on the floor, dragging himself closer to Patrice. "Patrice, help!" he let out before ultimately being sprawled on the floor.

Patrice paid no attention, and picked up her glass of merlot, swirling it around before gulping it down, and dabbing her mouth with her dinner cloth.

Melody looked over to Patrice, "What have you done?" she asked, "What have yo–". Slowly, Melody felt as her body let go, and she no longer had the power of her fingers and feet. She slid out of her chair attempting to get up, and run, but only made it to the doorway before her head grew too muffled, and her eyes closed to the world.

They were all out cold.

Chapter Forty

Melody woke up and she was no longer at the dinner table. The dim, gloomy setting of the dining room was replaced with the garden out back. Roses were in bloom, and the typical mist from the swamplands was replaced with clear, sunny skies. Everything looked brighter and happier. She walked down the pathway, to where her and Ashley usually sat, and watched her footsteps as she went. *One, two, three*, she counted as each one hit the stones.

...Seventy-nine, eighty. She finally reached the swing, and with it locked her eyes on a pair of brown dress shoes. Her eyes worked their way up the legs, then the hands and body, and settled on the face.

Melody's eyes grew wide with excitement, "Dad!" She leaped into his arms, and held him tight. "Oh, I've missed you so much,"

He smiled back, "I've missed you, too, sweetheart."

She pulled back from him, and looked back at the manor, "Wait, but where is everyone? How are you here? You're...you're...you're...," she couldn't spit out the words. Tears began to fall onto her purple blouse.

Dan lifted his hand and wiped the tears away, "Please don't cry, honey."

"I can't help it, Dad," she sobbed into his shoulder, "I wish you were real."

"I am real, I'm always with you—even when you can't see."

Melody sat down next to him, "Mom's selling the house, I couldn't stop her," she looked at the ground, and her voice wavered, "I'm sorry to let you down, Dad."

Dan placed his arm around her and he swung them gently back and forth.

"I could never be let down by you, sweetheart. I couldn't be more proud of the person you've become since I've been gone. The manor is just a place, it's not a representation of *us*."

Melody nodded; laying her head on his shoulder.

"Look at it as a new adventure."

"Nothing's an adventure with Patrice and Robert," she pretended to gag herself with her finger.

Dan playfully rolled his eyes, and they sat there swinging for a few moments.

"It's time for me to go now, love."

"Already? Please don't go!" Melody begged.

"Remember, I'm always here," he pointed at his heart, and his image faded.

"Wait, Dad, no!" Melody attempted to grab his hand one last time.

"Wake up, Mel!" he shouted to her. "Wake up!"

Melody paused, "Huh?"

Melody was getting shoved by Ashley. "Wake up, Mel!" Melody began to wake, but her head was hurting, and her body felt weak.

"What's going on? Where did Dad go?" Melody asked.

"What are you talking about?" Ashley's eyes looked fearful, "Mel, I think your mom drugged us at dinner!"

Melody jumped out of the bed, and her body hit the floor. Her legs were useless still from the drugs wearing off. "What is going on?" Her brain was still foggy, "I only remember seeing you...Oh, my god I remember your face hit the table and Robert..he tried to help you, but he passed out..." She rubbed her head, and tried to regain the strength in her legs. "That witch drugged us!"

"I've texted Reed, he's on his way," Ashley ran to the window, "Luckily, I left my phone in the room for dinner."

"On his way for what? It's not like we're in danger, she's just slightly loony," Melody suggested as reasoning for this behavior.

"Slightly loony? Mel, she's locked us in our room," Ashley pointed to the doorway, "Go on and try to open it."

Melody pulled with all her might to open the door.

"I told ya so. She's been down there shouting about how we all made her do this and that. She's lost her mind, Mel!" Ashley's anxiety was growing by the second as she paced the floor biting her nails. "What are we going to do?"

"I guess sit here and wait for Reed, are you able to fit through that window?"

Ashley rushed to the cracked window sill. She sucked in as far as she could, "Just barely, but I can do it," she replied back.

"Good, as soon as we see him in the distance, slide through there and go down the trellis, as long as she's not in the foyer we're good."

"What about Mara?" Ashley questioned.

"God dammit," Melody rolled her neck. "Tell Reed to stay at the end of the driveway until our signal. Let's go get Mara out of here."

Ashley maneuvered herself out onto the small roof. Melody was right behind her trying to pull through the opening. "Ash, I can't, it's too tight!" Go on without me! Go get help!"

"I am not leaving you now!" Ashley retaliated.

The doorknob to the room jiggled, and they looked at each other for what to do next.

"Hurry! Get in there!" Ashley said.

"You, go!"

Ashley ignored Melody's warnings and sucked her stomach in to get back in through the window. "Peanut butter and bologna always stick together." She grabbed Melody's hand and was yanked back into the room, with only seconds to spare before the door slowly opened.

A hand was seen first. It was unmanicured, and not the hand that they expected. Robert pulled himself into the room and closed the door behind him. Ashley cowered in the corner, and Melody blocked her with her own body. "Don't come any closer!"

Robert was in complete disarray. His hair was frazzled, and his dress shirt was coming out of his pants in different places. Melody's stance weakened, when she noticed the bruises on his face, and the slight drip of blood on his mouth.

"I'm not here to hurt you. I'm here to help you," he huffed from exhaustion. "I think she drank too much wine with her medications tonight and made them ineffective."

"Ineffective?" Melody repeated. "What medications?"

Robert slumped to the floor, pushing his hair back in the process. "Did you read the file?"

"The file?" Melody questioned again, "You were the one who slipped it under our door?" Her forehead grew lines at the idea.

"I had to, there was no other way for you to know what she's capable of."

Ashley composed herself, "But the file was from when she was sixteen. She was labeled cured with treatment."

"Yes, *cured with treatment*," Robert replied, "That's just it, she was cured with treatment, but when mixed with high doses of alcohol your mother can easily be tipped back into a psychosis."

"...There was a lot of alcohol today," Ashley observed.

"Preciously, Ashley," he put his head in his hands, "I don't know what to do. She's never gone this far with anything before."

"Before," asked Melody, "Are you implying my mother has done something similar in the past?"

"I mean, not to this extent, but yes," Robert looked through the keyhole, "You see, your mother and I, the plan wasn't to get married. I mean...it was, but then it wasn't," he stammered.

"What do you mean?" Melody asked, her voice dragging out while she tried to get more information from Robert.

"Errm, you weren't supposed to know, and it'd be off with my head for sure if *she* knew. Your mother and I, we did desire to be married in the beginning. Then things changed when I met Mara."

"Mara," Ashley repeated and looked to Melody with her usual doe eyes.

"Go on, we all know about your indiscretions with you teaching assistant, Robert," Melody huffed and folded her arms.

"Well, it started out small, and then turned into a relationship..." he paused.

"Go on, this is all stuff we know already," Melody began to pressure him.

"You know already? But how?"

Ashley held up the book she got from under her bed. The book with Mara and him pictured throughout.

"What is that?" Robert looked genuinely confused at the sight of the book. Melody took note and explained the contents to him, and handed it to him in the end. He flipped through the pages, and with each one his breath increased in pace. "Where did you get this?" His face looked cold and stern.

Melody yanked the book from his hands. "Your office. That's where. And we have enough evidence to assume you're the reason Mara's locked in the office," Melody shouted and as quickly as it escaped from her mouth, her hands were covering to keep more from falling out.

"What did you just say?" Robert questioned.

"Nothing!" Ashley piped up in the background.

"You *were* in the room with her the other night, weren't you?"

Ashley looked at Melody and gulped.

Melody glanced around the room for an alibi. Anything to take back what she said.

Robert brought himself up from the floor. "It's not what you think, I promise," he said as he stepped towards the girls.

Melody and Ashley retreated back.

Ashley slowly stepped back and crept out of the window. Melody grabbed the heavy brass lamp from the nightstand and wielded it as a weapon. "Stay back! We know everything you've done, and we're going to have the cops called to arrest you both!" Melody threatened.

"Me?" Robert pointed at himself. "Me! You really think it's all me?" He laughed at the idea, "Your mother has you all fooled. That book was from her trailing Mara and I after she found out about the affair. I threatened to leave her just like your dad did, and she threatened to blackball me and make me lose everything." He took another step forward, as Melody swung the lamp at him.

"I don't trust you!" Melody said.

Ashley stood on the roof with the wind blowing through her hair in the night breeze.

"Why would you trust me, your mother's done everything in her power to make me look like the bad guy," he paused for a second and thought about Reed, "I know you heard the story about your father and Annie, by now. Your mother planned it all!"

"That's what a killer would say!" Melody said as she inched to the window. "There's nothing you can say that would prove your innocence."

Robert stopped and looked around the room, "Melody, Mara went missing right after she told me she thought she might be pregnant. We were happy, and I was going to leave no matter the consequences. I wanted to be with Mara!"

Melody dropped the lamp in astonishment. "No..," she gasped.

"Your mother she's the one who kidnapped Mara. I had my suspicions, but they weren't based in reality until we came here. The first night your mother showed me what she did, and told me if I said *anything* she would kill her," Robert averted his eyes to the doorway, "There was no way to safely get her out without your mother knowing, Melody. I tried, and she has discovered the plans time and time again."

He fell to his knees and sobbed.

"It really wasn't you," she acknowledged. "And if that wasn't you, did you conspire with her to kill my father, so you could marry her?" Melody walked forward.

"KIll your father? I could never. He was my best friend."

"...Was it my mother?" Melody asked, but Robert was speechless. "Was it *my mother?*" Her tone grew more demanding to know the answer.

Robert hesitated at first and then nodded in agreement, "Yes," he whispered. "He wanted to leave her, too, because of her drinking and spending. Your father knew she had spent all of her fortune on the finer things, and he had already fallen for Annie again."

Melody turned to look at Ashley, who's mind was spinning at all of the new information being thrown at them. Ashley looked in the distance and saw Reed's lights, and pointed it out to Melody.

"Your mother didn't want him to leave, just like she doesn't want me to leave. After she blackmailed me into marriage, she told me the truth about your father, and how she was able to switch vials of trioxide from a cancer's patient's treatment plan, with a vial she had from the institution. Nobody at the hospital figured it out, as it all looked the same, but her old vial contained a less concentrated form."

Melody shook her head and pulled at her hair, not wanting to grasp everything she was hearing. "My mother killed my father...," the tears formed in her eyes.

Robert held her in his arms, "It's going to be okay, we just have to get out of here." He looked at the door, and held her by the shoulders. "Can you fit through that window?"

Melody trembled and shook her head no.

"I want you to listen to me. Ashley as soon as we leave this room, I want you to go down the trellis and start running for help. Melody, I'm going to check to assess the situation in the hall. I'll go first, and I want you to get to Mara and get her out of here. Go find help. Here's the key to her chains, I stole it from your mother." Robert looked in her eyes. "Do you understand me?"

Her eyes showed how she was breaking internally. Her body shaking; legs wanting to bow. "I...I...," she stuttered.

"Listen to me, you can do this. You are the most domineering person I know. If you can't, nobody can. Now, do you understand me?" He shook her shoulders to amp her up.

Melody nodded yes.

"Okay, good. Now let's go," he said as he walked to the door, and cracked it. He stepped out into the hallway and motioned for Melody to come out, and run to the bottom of the steps. She turned to face him before she ran, and noticed Patrice standing right behind him with a knife in her hand.

Melody screamed in fear, "Robert! Look out!"

Robert twisted to see what she was looking at, and was met with Patrice thrusting it into his back. "Run, Melody Run!" He shouted at her, as blood dripped on the floor—slowly at first and then a gush as she pulled the knife out. He collapsed to the floor. "Patrice, no!" he screamed.

Melody ran as fast as she could. She turned back once to watch in horror as Patrice stabbed him again, and his body went limp.

Chapter Forty One

Melody flew down the staircase. She ran to the foyer and stopped at the sliding door as she pushed the lion's head. The door slid open as she squeezed through and shut it in time before Patrice noticed where she went.

Melody looked through the peephole as she saw Patrice walking through with the knife in her hand. Robert's blood was smeared on it, and Patrice looked crazier than ever. Her eyes were wild, and her normally taken care of extensions were falling from her hair. Melody put her back against the wall to catch her breath.

"Melody!" Patrice yelled. "Get out here right now!"

The fear welled up inside of her for the first time this entire trip. Her own mother had betrayed the family. Patrice had single handedly killed her father for money and saving face from a divorce. A lump in her throat formed, but she tried to hold it in.

"Melody!" Patrice's voice grew shriller. She was on the hunt to finish what she started, and leave no rock unturned. Melody watched as she went through each room looking for her.

Patrice came from the kitchen, and her demeanor had softened. "Oh, Melody, I'm sorry honey. Mama's just had too much to drink, darling. Please come out, I just want to protect you from that insane man," she cooed. Patrice stopped and looked around. She picked up a vase and slammed it to the floor. "Melody! I am tired of these games. Get out here, right now!" She snapped as she ran down the hallway.

Melody choked on the tears she was attempting to hold in. She gathered her nerves and ran up the steps to Mara. She pulled the key from her pants and put it into the hole, turning it as fast as she could to open. Melody entered the room, Mara was hiding in the corner they had last seen her. "Listen, we don't have much time, but we have to go now!" Melody pulled out the key Robert gave her and undid Mara's chains.

Mara stood up, and together they ran out of the room and Melody heard the lock from the other side. Melody locked their side of the passage and they descended the staircase.

"Where's Robert? Is he okay," Mara cried out.

"I..I don't know," Melody admitted. She pulled Mara's arm and they made their way to the opening. "Once we are out in the open we need to run to the front door. It's a straight walk, and only about fifty feet ahead. Mara, you need to run to the end of the driveway where you'll find Ashley."

Mara screamed, "She did this to me! And now she's hurt Robert!" Mara began to grow erratic as she processed everything. "First me, and now Robert," she wailed. Mara said as she fell to the floor in a heap of tears. "How could she do this?"

Melody knelt down to her, and placed her hand on her shoulder. "I don't know, Mara. But I do know this: She's not going to hurt us if I have anything to say about it." She lifted Mara off of the ground and recomposed herself. "Now, I want you to run as fast as you can and get Ashley, do you read me?"

Mara wiped the tears away and braced herself as Melody opened the door. She ran to the doorway and flung open the door with Melody close behind. Mara was out in the open and running down the driveway towards Reed's lights, when Melody looked to her right and saw Patrice charging at her from a distance. Melody quickly shut the front door to give Patrice a pause in her step and she took off down the driveway.

Melody ran as fast as her feet could carry her, and she soon caught up to Mara who was stumbling from not using her legs for months. She put her arm under Mara's shoulder and helped support her as they got to Reed's car. Reed jumped out and grabbed Mara, who jumped back in fear initially.

"It's okay, Mara, he's safe. He just wants to help," Ashley spoke gently to her.

Mara listened and was helped into the car. Melody jumped into the passenger seat, as Reed got back in.

They all gathered a breath, as they realized that Patrice was standing before them in the bright high beams. Blood stains on her dress and face, and the knife placed by her side, as she cocked her head to the side and smiled.

Patrice lunged at the car, as Melody slammed Reed's leg down on the gas, "Go!"

The car sped in reverse as they hightailed it onto the road to town. Patrice ran after them until they could no longer see them. Melody took a deep breath in, and exhaled out, and with it a flood of emotions as she attempted to understand the unfolding events.

Reed was the first one to break the silence, "What the hell is going on?" He demanded to know.

Ashley locked eyes with him from the backseat. *Are you okay*, he mouthed. She shook her head yes, and reached for his hand. He squeezed it tight and kissed it.

"Well, you see, the liquor. It finally got to Patrice," Melody joked.

"This is no time for jokes, Mel!" Ashley stressed.

Melody waved it off. "I know, I just don't really know what to say."

"At least give me the highlights," Reed suggested.

"Well, let's see. I watched Robert get stabbed after he admitted that my mom killed my father for his money, I saved Mara from the crypt, Patrice has lost her mind because she drank while on her insanity medications, and well...." The lump in Melody's throat formed again and Melody pushed it back down. "Is that enough information, yet?"

Reed went quiet, and drove on. "Where am I supposed to go?" He asked. "The police station is a one man show in this town, and he's out of office until morning."

"Drive to your house, Patrice won't think to look there," Melody said.

They all sat in silence, not knowing what to do or say. They all had bore witness to a horrible sight that night, and they were all bound by this situation. Melody was losing her family piece by piece, and while getting rid of Robert had been her goal at the beginning of the summer, she certainly didn't want it to have happened the way it did.

"Mel, is Robert...is he dead?" Ashley inquired.

"I think so," Melody whispered back. She peered out the window as the trees disappeared and the little shops sprouted up. Soon they turned onto a dirt path, and down a winding road in the middle of nowhere. The car pulled up to a small cottage that blended into the wooded scenery. Melody could see Mrs. Annie inside cooking a meal on the stove, as she bent down to taste the stew she was making. The warm lights were inviting and Melody felt relieved to be in a safe place, for now. She worried about what Patrice would do if she found them, but attempted to block it out of her mind for the time being. *What am I going to do,* she asked herself.

Chapter Forty Two

Annie noticed Reed's car pulled up, and rushed outside when she realized every seat was filled. The signature mom look of panic had set in and the wrinkles near her eyes became more visible.

Melody opened up her door, and Reed stepped out.

"Are you guys okay? Isn't it a little late to be out right now?" Annie asked.

Reed put his hand up, "Mom, please stop with the questioning." He walked to Ashley's door and opened it for her.

Ashley stepped out, and held the frame of the car, "...We're all fine, now that we're here...but I think we need your help to figure out what to do." Ashley looked at Annie and then turned her eyes to Mara in the backseat. Annie peeked in to see, and gasped at the sight.

Mara's wrists were covered in bruises, and her white night gown had been soiled from her own urine. Her feet were covered in dirt and leaves, and her hair was matted; unbrushed for months.

"Is she okay?" Annie hesitated, "Who is that?"

"We'll tell you inside," Melody motioned, and everybody got to the door as Ashley coaxed Mara out. She was skittish and didn't like the new scenery, but she didn't feel as unsafe anymore.

Nervously, she walked the steps and made sure to keep her distance from the others.

Melody sat down at the dinner table and looked around. The home was small and quaint with an open floor plan that allowed for space for the living and dining rooms to be merged as one. To the left was the small kitchen with the stove, sink, and refrigerator pushed to one side, leaving enough room for the small island in the center. Melody smiled. It reminded her of a simple environment. It didn't look as if they had more than they needed, but that it was mostly filled with love. She looked at the walls that were filled with pictures of Reed and Annie. One stood out from the rest, that was placed gingerly on the small fireplace that had been converted to a pellet stove. Melody stood up and walked over to pick it up. In the frame was her dad with Annie. It looked like a high school picture, as Annie leaned into Dan, both with big smiles showing each tooth. Annie was wearing a short floral dress; her fingers making the peace sign as she blew a kiss to the camera. Dan in a blue Yale sweater; his dark hair parted down the middle.

Melody softly smiled at the idea of their happiness, until she remembered the situation at hand. Annie had come back in from rounding everyone into the living room, and Melody watched as Ashley comforted Mara.

Reed had his eyes to the ground, and when Melody came around the corner to the kitchen island, he looked at her waiting for her to tell him what to do or say. Melody looked at Annie, "We have a problem."

Melody told Annie everything, about the entire summer wanting to solve a mystery and how she hoped to get rid of Robert. How she found the arsenic and scrapbook and attempted to make Patrice and

Robert confess to Dan's death or Mara's whereabouts. Then things go quiet for a moment as Annie digested all of the findings before that night. Reed held his mom's hand to lower the stress, and Melody went into what happened.

"Mom...Patrice...I don't even know what I want to call her anymore. She drugged everyone at dinner, locked Ashley and me in our room, and Robert came to find us. That's when Ashley texted Reed to come help us, and I couldn't fit through the window," Melody explained.

Annie poured everybody hot tea from her kettle and placed a loving hand on Melody as she filled hers. "I think we need to call the cops, dear. They need to arrest them."

Melody shook her head no. "There is no *them* anymore. I don't think Robert made it out."

Annie placed her hand on her mouth in shock. "What do you mean?"

"Robert unlocked the door for us, and we confronted him face-to-face about the vial and book...he had never seen the book before, and was surprised we knew about him and Mara. I don't think he had anything to do with it all. He explained mom's time in the institute and then told us how she....," Melody couldn't spit out the rest as she hid her face.

Annie looked at her son for answers, "Patrice killed Dan because she wanted the money from his death since she spent her fortune. Robert knew and was blackmailed into marriage." Reed paused, and came in with the final doozy, "Now Robert's dead, because he wanted to leave."

"Oh my, heavens! That's it. I'm calling the police right now," she said as she picked up the phone from the wall and started calling. "Yes, hello, Sheriff Rollins," she waited for the Sheriff to finish his words, "Yes, I know it's late on a weekend, but I think you need to get down here to my place. There's been a murder down at the Meltront Manor." Annie paused again, and continued, "No, no, Melody and the other girl both are here...and it seems they have someone else as well," Annie held her head as the Sheriff kept cutting her off. "No, I think you need to come see it for yourself. Bring back up, bring the medics. I think they've found your missing woman."

Annie hung up the phone and looked back for the teenagers. All of the seats were empty and Mara and Ashley were no longer on the couch. "Now where could they have gotten to?" Annie mumbled.

Annie glanced outside only to see the kids begging someone for something. She stepped out onto her porch with a knife in hand. "What are you guys doing out here? You–" Annie was interrupted as she realized what they were all begging for. Her eyes met with the eyes of a frazzled blonde in a ripped black Versace dress. Makeup was smeared on her face, and in her arms she had Mara.

Patrice gripped Mara tight and had her knife against the teaching assistant's throat. "You've ruined everything, yet again, and I need to fix it as always," she sneered.

Mara's eyes widened in pain as Patrice nicked her throat and a small droplet of blood escaped. Her hands reached out for someone to help.

Reed looked back at his mom, "Help! What do we do?"

Annie froze in her spot, unsure of how to handle the situation. She formed her grip on the knife, and took a step forward.

Chapter Forty Three

Patrice held the knife without wavering.

"Mom, please, stop this!" Melody shouted. She placed a hand out and tried to step forward.

"Here goes Melody, always wanting to be the hero in the story. Always off on her little detective games. Well, this time you've gone too far," Patrice mocked as she swiped the knife at the group, "Now, back up!"

Annie mustered what courage she could while having a madwoman in the driveway. She took a step forward, her hands out in defensive mode. "Patrice, it's not worth it. Put the knife down."

Patrice laughed, "Not worth it? Not worth it she says. Funny coming from the homewrecker. Was it worth Dan's life for the fleeting romance?" She questioned.

"Why did you kill Dan?" Annie asked as she took another step forward.

"Because of you. You two were going to ruin my self-image I worked so hard for. All I could picture were how wild the tabloids would get about a "sad Patrice" in the wake of a divorce," Patrice chorted, "And I could never be sad over something as pathetic as Dan, who would never choose the finer things in life—despite having the money for it."

Tears formed in Melody's eyes. Her mother was cold and callous. Traits that she had always seen, but now she saw her mother's vanity front and center. It was her biggest flaw and the one that would penultimately take her down. Ashley held Melody on the porch, as she was ready to run at her mother and take her down, "Let me go," Melody argued.

"I'm not going to let you willingly get hurt," Ashley pleaded.

Reed walked to the left while everybody focused on Patrice. Annie had her in a staredown, and he took advantage to get closer to the knife.

"You killed him because he didn't want to spend his money?" Annie took another step.

"No, I killed him because he wanted you. That would've meant that I would be penniless and humiliated. We couldn't have that could we?" Patrice pouted. "If I couldn't have him, do you really think I would've allowed scum like you to have him?"

"You didn't have to kill him, Patrice. Now this poor girl, who's already lost her father, is going to lose her mother when you go to jail," Annie admitted.

"Me in jail? You're mistaken. They wouldn't believe you over me. Money talks sweetheart, and I own every cop in tow—"

Patrice was cut off as Mara and Reed locked eyes. Mara elbowed Patrice in the stomach and caught her off guard.

"You little bitch!" Patrice yelled as she chased after Mara.

Reed came from behind and knocked the knife out of her hand. Patrice gripped her wrist in pain, and lunged again for the knife. The girls ran inside as they waited for Annie and Reed to come back up the steps to safety.

"That little no good brat was never good enough to be at the top of society like me," she said as she stood up and brushed the dust off of her dress. Her top lip was cracked and a small pool of blood formed. Patrice looked in front of her and saw the knife only three feet away. She glanced at Reed and then at Annie before running for the knife.

Annie knew what she had to do and raced for the knife.

Patrice got to it first, and picked it up ready to stab it into Annie.

"The world's going to find out everything you did, Patrice. They'll finally see the monster you always were," Annie taunted.

Patrice stopped and smiled, the blood on her face started to crust and crack. "Oh, that's not the story they're going to know." She swung the knife at Annie, and teased her, "My goodness, Mr. Sheriff. That crazy book lady was stalking us this whole summer," her eyes growing wild.

Annie stepped back as Patrice took another swing, "And how do you propose to explain the kids' testimonies? They'll still be alive to tell the truth?"

"Oh, don't worry about them, I can finish them before that time comes."

Patrice began to run at Annie with the knife above her head.

Annie screamed, and shielded her face with her arms.

POW!

A single gunshot was all that was heart, as Annie realized Patrice was no longer running. She opened her eyes and looked before her as Patrice was standing over her.

Patrice looked down at her chest and saw blood forming on her dress, "The dry cleaners are going to have a hard time with that one," she expressed as she fell to the ground. The blood pooled around her.

Annie stood up in her spot and looked around for the owner of the gun. In the distance she saw Sheriff Rollins point down the shotgun.

Rollins walked up to Patrice's body. His brown work boot gently pushed against her as he waited for her to move. When she didn't stir, he moved to her front and verified her death.

"Didn't come a moment too soon," Annie complained.

"I came as fast as I could," he replied as he averted his eyes to his white shirt and jeans to show her.

More squad cars pulled in, and the sound of the ambulances were off in the near distance. Sheriff Rollins stepped inside and heard the story of the sounds in the wall and Patrice's confessions. He called a sheriff in New York to confirm Mara's identity and explain to them that she was found to which they immediately dispatched cars to come take her home. Mara was put into the back of Rollins' personal vehicle and waited there shaking from everything she had experienced. *It's finally over*. She looked out at the sight of the flashing lights and closed her eyes to rest.

Chapter Forty Four

The rest of the tragic night was a blur for Melody and Ashley, who were whisked away to the hospital to be checked out. Bernie and Annie both came to the hospital to check on them and ensure that they were okay. Reed, who had lunged at Patrice, was treated for his mild lacerations on his hands as a result of the scuffle, and was checked out within hours.

Both the girls and Mara's stay were lengthened to allow for psychological evaluations. Ashley checked out fine, but Melody was flagged for PTSD. Melody laughed it off, because she knew she was better off without a mother than with one that never valued her for more than the dollar signs she saw in her place.

The girls drove back with Bernie and Ashley's mother to gather their remaining things from the manor. They had been told the place was a crime scene and needed to be investigated before anyone could enter, so there they left all their possessions.

Bernie looked in the rearview mirror at the girls, "I do hope you two have been handling things okay," he sympathized.

Ashley picked at her fingers and looked out the window at the passing swamps.

Ashley's mother, Clara, reached back from the passenger seat to hold her daughter's hand. Her brown hair swirled around her nude face. "Please, forgive her, she's had a rough time about coming back to this place.""No need to apologize, I understand," Bernie replied.

After ten minutes, Melody looked up to Bernie, "Mara's going to be here, right?"

"That's right, Ms. Melody."

"And Reed and Mrs. Annie, as well?"

"Yes, Ms. Melody," he paused and looked back, "And I hope you don't mind, but I also invited Mr. Drewmore to the estate as well."

Ashley's eyes turned inquisitive, the brown reflecting all of her thoughts. "Mr. Drewmore? You mean—"

Bernie smiled in the mirror, "He's alive."

"But how? Mom definitely stabbed him a few times until he stopped moving," Melody pondered.

"Luckily, she managed to miss the most vital of arteries and his heart, which allowed for a slower bleed. When they found him, he was turning cold but he managed to stabilize him for transport."

Melody smiled, "You know this whole summer—and the past few years—I've always hated Robert, because I associated him with my father's death, and with the upheaval of our family," she looked out at the trees as they turned into the driveway. "Turns out the real devil was next to me all along parading around as a mother that cared. I guess he never really was a monster."

Ashley grabbed her hand and squeezed it, "I always told you to give him a chance, Mel."

"I know, goon."

The car drove around the fountain and then parked in front of the stairs leading to the front. Melody saw Merna standing at the open window facing the driveway, and the doorway opened as Robert, Annie, and Reed rushed out. The way the sun reflected off of the manor's gray walls made it illuminate in a way that made it not as dreary, but more of an artwork, and Melody understood why her father had loved it so much.

When the car stopped, and just as he had when they first got there he walked to their doors and opened it up for them to get out. He placed his arm around Melody's shoulder and walked her to the group.

"You're a brave girl, and your father would be so proud of you," Bernie whispered. He took his place next to those Melody had wanted to be there for the occasion, and watched as Melody looked around the outside grounds one last time.

Melody inhaled, gathering all the bravery she could once more. "My father first brought me here fifteen years ago, and with it it has brought me both good and bad memories. I'll always cherish the time I got to spend here with each and every one of you," she hesitated as she looked at Robert, "And I guess I even appreciate the memories, this summer, with you as I solved my first real mystery," she gently smiled.

"Mine too," Ashley chimed in with a laugh.

"As I look back on everything that happened here, I see how it's changed me, and frankly, I don't want this lifestyle. Maybe in a few years, after I graduate college, I can come back to this place and see it in a new light where it can hold a place in my goals. Maybe it won't—who knows. What I do know is that I wouldn't be myself without the guidance of you two," Melody said as she placed one hand each to Bernie and Merna. "You two have been my safe haven for fifteen years, and I thank you for that. Dad's will made sure that you two were taken care of, and due to Patrice's untimely death, I have been allowed to see it through. You both will be compensated to stay with the manor as long as you choose."

Merna gasped and wept at the notion that she would be taken care of. Bernie wrapped his arms around Melody, "I was right, he's definitely proud of you Ms.... I mean Melody," he gave one more tight squeeze and then recomposed himself into the butler position.

Melody walked to Annie and Reed.

"Mrs. Annie, I know that things would have been much different, if my father were still alive. You saved Ashley and I—and Mara—from certain death. You loved my father for who he was and not his money," Melody's eyes misted at the thought. "I know that he would want this place to be used for good, and even though I detest books, my best friend over here says they're good for something," she turned to crack a smile at Ashley.

Ashley clapped her hands in excitement at what was to come.

"That's why I wish to leave you with the manor to turn a part of it into a new storefront for your bookstore, but you can also repurpose with Merna and Bernie into a bed and breakfast. I hear murder mysteries are all the rage right now for themed lodges." Melody hugged Annie and Ashley ran up to Reed jumping in his arms. "Yuck," Melody gagged at their relationship.

One last time Melody walked the halls of the manor. The walls didn't feel as sticky from the summer heat, and all signs of the dust had worn away. She walked to the office she had been forbidden to go near all summer, and sat herself at the desk as she reclined in the swivel chair. Spinning one last time, imagining that she was on her father's lap laughing at the magic of childhood.

Melody had solved the mystery she had wanted to solve all along. It might not have been the one she had set out to complete in June, but it qualified just the same. She knew that she wouldn't be back here for years, while she finished high school and moved on to university. But she knew she'd be back sometime. Maybe in a few decades when she started a family—*who truly knows the path of one's life*, Melody thought.

The next adventure awaited, and with it Melody would be ten steps ahead on the hunt for a new mystery.

ABOUT THE AUTHOR

Bea lives with her husband and two children in Pennsylvania. She received her BA in English from Millersville University and completed her MA in English and Creative Writing at Southern New Hampshire University. When she's not at school or taking care of her children, she is always thinking of her next story and prefers to write in the genres of mystery and young adult. *Manor* was previously published as a *Kindle Vella*.

Melody and Ashley walked around the campus of Millersville University. The large campus was bustling with students moving into their new spaces for the year, and Ashley grew anxious looking at the map.

"Okay, so I found our hall! It's right here, and we're–" Ashley was looking for a building signage to direct them: **The Sugar Bowl**, "we're over here...," her voice trailed off after realizing they were on the opposite side of campus.

"Goon, I told you we should have just gone where the largest groups were getting off the bus." Melody looked to see how far they'd have to drag their luggage. "That's it. I give up, let's just stop here for a moment and grab something to eat. You know, reconvene or something."

"I guess so. It is really hot, and should definitely rehydrate."

"Yea, yea. Water this, and water that," Melody rolled her eyes.

The girls went inside the campus diner and grabbed a menu. A boy of about his early twenties stopped at their table to take their orders. His skin was tan, and his blue eyes were intriguing to Melody. Ashley looked across the table and gave Melody the secret look for a cute boy.

"Hi, I'm Mario, but you can call me M. I'll be helping to get you fed," he joked with a smile.

Ashley ordered a slice of pizza, and Melody...she froze for the first time in her life around the opposite sex. "Ummm, she'll just take the same as me," Ashley answered for Melody.

M gave a chuckle and walked to put the order in. Melody sat at the table with her face in her hands shaking her head back and forth from embarrassment. Within ten minutes two slices of pizza and fries were put onto their table.

'Oh, we didn't order any fries," Ashley stated.

"Don't worry, they're actually on the house," M replied looking at Melody. "I hope you enjoy it."

"You too!" Melody stammered out.

"I will!" M said as he turned around laughing to himself.

Melody's face grew redder by the second as she realized her words. "This isn't going to be my year," she grumbled.

"Don't worry, no year has been my year yet," Ashley joked.

Melody gave an annoyed look, "Says the one who's been in a steady long-term relationship with Mr. Reed."

"What do you care about in the dating department?"

"I don't, and I don't plan to want to learn anytime soon," Melody said seriously.

"Ah, yes. There's the Mel I know and love. So cynical." Ashley dipped her fry into ketchup.

Melody looked out the window toward the student dorms again. This time she noticed a small figure in a window. *What is that? Is someone putting in an air conditioner? I thought we couldn't bring our own!* Melody thought.

Then the figure moved and four appendages appeared as she realized it was a person in the window.

She turned back to Ashley, "Hey, do you see that over there?"

"Where?" Ashley shielded her eyes from the sun and attempted to see what Melody was looking at.

"There, at the dorms, about ten floors up." Melody pointed in the direction.

"Yea, I see it. It's probably just someone trying to hang up some curtains.

Melody kept looking at the figure as it danced in the window, and Ashley finished her pizza while taking in the scenery of the fast paced life of college around her.

Moments later, everybody's phones went off at the same time: **Alert: Code Blue. Please stay where you are until further advisement.**

Ashley looked up from her phone only to see Melody dashing out the diner and across the campus.

"Hey, you didn't pay!" M ran around the cash register shouting.

"So sorry!" Ashley attempted to apologize as she ran after Melody, "I promise we'll be right back!"

M looked to the table and noticed all of their luggage was still there, which helped ease his mind from thinking he'd be stiffed.

Melody ran the distance in no time, and stood at the garden below the tall, 20-story dormitory. The green grass was neatly trimmed, and the foliage around campus was changing from summer to fall. She looked around her and only saw a small group of students watching the girl in the window above. *They must've been the ones to call*, she observed.

Ashley came up from behind her panting from exhaustion. "How do you run like that, when you don't even exercise?" she huffed.

"Shh, no time for that now," Melody said as she pointed to the open window. I want to know what she's doing."

"Well, you go up and find out, because I'm out of breath. I'll wait for you down here."

Melody used her id to get in through the door, and made her way up to the floor the girl was on. "Now which door," she whispered. She looked up and down the hallway trying to figure out which door the girl was behind. One stood out from the rest as it was just slightly cracked.

She slowly entered the room only to notice that the girl wasn't alone. Behind her was a figure in black. Slender in size, from what Melody could tell as they wore a pair of black jogger pants and hooded sweatshirt.

Just as she was going to say something, Melody watched helplessly as the girl jumped from the window. She ran up to the window, and looked down below. The girl's body splayed out on the concrete sidewalk.

Ashley let out a loud scream, and security came running out of the woodwork. Only several feet away lay the body of a girl they never knew. Her hair mixed with the blood that poured out of her skull and into the pores of the concrete. Ashley looked at the poor girl, with her eyes wide open and her jaw dislocated from the fall. Not one body part was in its correct location as they twisted and turned in multiple directions. She looked away, just as Melody quickly turned around to confront the figure in black.

Melody saw them as they ran out of the room and down the hallway. Trying to chase after them she noticed the elevator was set to floor two, and she dashed down the stairwell to beat them to their destination.

She made it just in time to see the doors to the elevator sliding open, and Melody lunged to shove the perpetrator, but there was nobody there. Melody looked around the floors and realized she had been tricked.

Making her way back outside, she grabbed Ashley as everybody's eyes diverted to them. "She didn't do that on her own," Melody told Ashley as they briskly walked to the Sugar Bowl.

Cop cars quickly filled the residences and started asking questions to the group of students outside the hall. One student pointed at Melody and Ashley as their backs were facing them. "The girl fell, and that girl on the left was staring out the window after," she cried.

The rest of the group tried to calm the spectator down, as the cops made their way to Melody who was now gathering her items, while Ashley paid for their meals.

"Hello, ma'am. We'd like to bring you into the station for questioning," he said sternly.

Melody gave a look of distress as the cops escorted her from the diner and to the backseat of their car. Ashley ran out the door, to watch as Melody was taken away.

Made in the USA
Middletown, DE
17 April 2024

53007543R00120